For Andre Schlessinger, New York's original punk rock detective.

Rest In Peace.

Acknowledgements

Garry Bushell: I wrote this book mainly between 2023 and 2024. I would have finished it sooner, but work got in the way. Thanks to Darren Laws and Caffeine Nights for their patience and to my family and friends for their encouragement. Question everything. Stay free.

June 2025.

Craig Brackenridge: dedicated to the Black Puma. Rest in peace, brother. Keep rockin'.

Caffeine Nights Publishing

BAD APPLE

Harry Tyler In New York
by

GARRY BUSHELL

With
CRAIG BRACKENRIDGE

 Fiction aimed at the heart and the head…

Published by Caffeine Nights Publishing 2025

Published in England by
Caffeine Nights Publishing
Amity House
71 Buckthorne Road
Minster on Sea
Isle of Sheppey
ME12 3RD

caffeinenights.com
caffeinenightsbooks.com

Printed in England by CMP (uk) Limited
Also available as an eBook

British Library Cataloguing in Publication Data
A CIP catalogue record for this book is available from the British Library

ISBN: 978-1-913200-36-7

Everything else by
Default, Luck and Accident

You never know when betrayal will come. Even if you are highly skilled at assuming other guises, it doesn't mean that you can always detect when someone else is playing the same game. The hard, cold shock of the unexpected twist hits you like an ice bucket challenge.

Chapter 1

It didn't look much from the outside, but at least the Double Down Saloon had laid on some entertainment. Through the window, I saw the young goth barmaid duck for cover as a fist the size of a pork knuckle slammed straight and hard into Andre Schweitzer's shoulder. It was meant for his chin, but he'd dodged it like a seasoned flyweight. He couldn't swerve the punch from the other guy though. His second opponent – a big bulky fella who looked like Rocky Balboa on a deep-fried rhino diet – sunk a solid right deep into Andre's guts, taking the wind right out of his sails.

That had to hurt.

I walked in, rounding up the clientele to four.

'How ya doin', partner?' I said amiably. 'Who are your girlfriends?'

'Butt out of this,' Rocky snarled. He had one gold tooth and two missing ones, his gut was threatening to bust out of his cheap whistle, and his face was pocked like a Biggin Hill gravel road. The bloke looked as happy as a scrapyard Rottweiler who hadn't been fed for a fortnight.

The barmaid's face crept back up. She was young, early 20s, and tears of fear had smeared her cheeks with spindly spiders' legs of black mascara. An out-of-towner was my guess. She would grow up fast in this joint.

Rocky stepped towards me. I didn't move. The big lug threw a left in my direction. It was a good punch, hard and vicious, but like the cogs in his brain, it was way too slow. Crocky, you might say. By the time it landed, in mid-air behind my right ear, I had kicked in his kneecap.

It must have stung something rotten. You would have heard the echoes of the crack if he hadn't screamed so loud.

Funny how a big man can squeal like a teenybopper pissing her pubescent panties over Lee Ryan at a Blue concert.

His bald, belligerent, red-faced buddy – let's call him Tubby Savalas – started coming my way, spitting steam like the dinosaur that killed Wayne Knight in Jurassic Park. I side-stepped, and he slammed straight into the bar. The force of the impact made the wood visibly shudder, and the poor barmaid ducked out of sight again...

'Who luvs ya, baby?' I asked, trying to wind him up.

I figured he would go for one of two responses – either he'd charge back straight at me or he'd reach inside his jacket. I moved forwards, anticipating the latter, trying to get close enough to disarm him. I wasn't quick enough.

'You cock-sucker!' Tubby growled as he pulled a girlie Glock 43 out of his jacket pocket. I grabbed a beer bottle as he aimed the gun straight at me. Or I should say, as he attempted to aim it straight at me. Before the bottle had left my hand, Andre had smashed him over the canister with a frosted pint pot.

Tubby went down like Goliath in the Valley of Elah.

'You have a nice day,' I said.

I turned to Andre, who was panting. His face was a mess of sweat and blood – he looked like Bruce Willis in the last half-hour of any Die Hard film.

'Thanks man,' he said. He was wheezing hard, fighting for breath. His heart was pounding, his mouth was dry, and his face was as bruised as a badly juggled peach in a concrete car park.

'Drink?'

'Yeah, bro, but maybe not here,' he said, attempting to clean up his kisser with the sleeve of his retro Harrington Jacket. 'Let's go.'

I nodded. 'Suits me.'

Andre's cell-phone rang, right on cue. He answered. 'Yeah…thanks…it just happened…no, I'm fine…Oh really… Yeah, just leaving, thanks again.'

He looked at me and shrugged. 'That was Buster, my cop pal, telling me to get the hell out of Dodge. I'll explain all this when we're in more convivial surroundings.'

I shrugged. I didn't care where I drank as long as I drank. It had been a long day, and I needed a livener. Waving goodbye to the barmaid, we stepped out onto Avenue A into an unexpected New York downpour. It had been sunny when I walked in, now the rain was coming down like stair rods – straight and hard, and nearly as mean as the city.

'Lovely. Pissing down like a camel with two cunts,' I said.

Andre grunted. 'The two cunts are back in the bar.'

'Will the barmaid call the cops?'

'They are the cops. Clapp and Delaney. How do you say it back home – "bent as a nine-bob note",' He paused. 'How do I look?'

I studied him. 'Like something vaguely supernatural that just staggered out of a vandalised ghost train… the pasty white Chevy, the red trails of claret… it's all very Hammer Horror, mate, very in vogue. Here y'are, use this.'

I handed him my handkerchief. He wiped the blood off, letting the rain clean his face; then he flagged down a yellow cab and muttered something incomprehensible.

Muhammad put his foot down, and we left Union Market behind, heading for the more Celtic shenanigans of McSorley's Old Ale House less than a mile away on East 7th Street. Mo's wipers were going like a pair of hyperactive metronomes.

I glanced casually out of the corner of my eye and noticed that a dark blue Chrysler sedan was two cars behind. Five will get you ten that it was the same dark blue Chrysler sedan that had been trailing either me or him or both of us for the past two days.

Three cars behind that, was a beaten-up yellow Volks Wagon campervan that had been hanging around since yesterday and was harder to miss.

'Looks like we got ourselves a convoy,' I said.

'The usual?'

'Yeah.'

'Amateurs.'

He finished wiping his face with my handkerchief, blew his nose on it, and tried to give it back. I pushed it away.

'Not even if you boiled it, you skank.'

'Skank. That doesn't mean Yank, does it? That's septic, septic tank.'

'Ho! I taught you well.'

'But Chevy, you said earlier. Presumably Chevy Chase is face. I thought that was boat, as in boat race.'

'It is. They're both right, both mean face. I just thought you'd appreciate a friendly septic reference. Plus, I watched Caddyshack again last week.'

'I need to study harder. Caddyshack one, I take it.'

'Course! The sequel stank like Satan's khazi.'

'A waste of Jackie Mason.'

The cab pulled over. The ride had taken under four minutes, yet the torrent of rain had dwindled to a light drizzle.

'If you ever do an Irish pub crawl here, this is the first stop on the Blarney Chain,' said Andre. He handed Mo a five-buck tip on top of the fare while glancing discreetly at the tailing vehicles as that drove on by. 'They've got Guinness on tap and Houdini's handcuffs are locked to a bar rail, courtesy of Harry himself. And oh, and if anyone asks, you're Australian.'

'No worries, mate,' I replied in slow, cod-Aussie, sounding for all the world like Crocodile Dundee after a seizure.

'Some of our plastic Paddies don't take kindly to the Brits.'

'Received and reciprocated. Some of us bonzer Brits didn't take kindly to your plastic Paddies funding the fucking Provos for years on end. Now, are you going to tell me what all that was about?'

'I was about to, because as it happens, you're to blame.'

Well, that figured.

I sighed. The curse of the big bad apple. It had all started so well, too.

***

People didn't tend to notice Kevin Malone much, and those that did would normally lower their eyes or turn away. There was something of the mortuary attendant about him – the few words, the air of funereal woe, the whiff of formaldehyde. His friends called him the Angel of Death. The fourth generation Bostonian Irishman watched the limey and bald prick walk out of the Double Down, and then found a pay phone and dialled. The call was answered, but nobody spoke.

'It's me,' he said in his dull monotone.

'Talk.'

'Your guy was there, as expected. The off-duty feds turned up and were working him over good. Then his buddy showed.'

'English?'

'Yeah. Cockney.'

'Result?'

'Two KOs. The Keystone cops, out for the count.'

At the other end of the line, a man wearing a Rolex Oyster and a $30,000 diamond encrusted gold bracelet, sucked on his Cohiba Maduro 5 Magicos and laughed.

'Good,' he said. The off-duty policemen would be paid for their efforts and compensated for their injuries later. In his experience, all New York cops were for sale, but these two out-of-shape veterans were small-time. Grazers. Happy for a few bucks and the odd favour. The Hunters, the more aggressive kind, are hungrier and cost a whole lot more. But they're worth it.

Anyhow, message sent. The bald pain-in-the-ass private dick will know it was a warning, and the Englishman will be rattled. Maybe so rattled he would cut short his trip. Why stay? Hanging around would be extremely bad for his health. They had done what was necessary, and now Tyler needed to be encouraged to leave. Either of his own accord in first class luxury or in a wooden box. He blew out a stream of cigar smoke and shrugged his broad shoulders before reaching for a mirror and a razor blade.

Alive or dead, what's the difference?

He had to be more careful with Schweitzer. Connections and circumstances. Temporary complications.

He thought about things for a moment, looked at his watch, and made another call.

'I want background on the English prick. As much as you can get as quick as you can get it. Any dirt, any weaknesses.'

'Already done,' a crisp Home Counties British voice replied. 'He's a womaniser, a libertine, so…'

'Got it. So we'll set a trap to catch a rat. A love rat.'

Chapter 2

Two days earlier
Monday 12th May, Midtown Manhattan

'Wake up, sleepy head.'

A woman. A hand shook me and I groaned slightly. I opened one eye and tried to take in my surroundings. The clock said 5:02. My head felt like the cast of Riverdance were rehearsing inside it. What? Where? Who? Why?

Another shake. I smelt perfume. Delicious DKNY?

The fragrance belonged to whoever I was in bed with. I felt the warmth of her body, the hand lingering on my shoulder, her breasts pushing softly against my back.

'Come back to the land of the living…'

The voice was English. It had started life in the Home Counties but had been seasoned with years of overseas travel. Umm.

'Come on,' she said, adding a mockney 'Urry up, Arry.'

I cursed Jimmy Pursey for approximately the seventy-seven thousandth time in my life, then I turned and smiled.

She was easy to smile at.

Blonde, with a perfect snub nose, eyes like pure-set honey and a smile that could melt a cheese roll fifteen paces. Holy moly. Who was she? The woman was younger than me by about ten years and drop dead gorgeous to boot. She looked like a young Elizabeth Montgomery. Think! Think… yeah. Finally, the brain-cells kicked in. She was the First Class stewardess on my British Airways flight into JFK yesterday.

'Hello you.'

T. Her name had started with a T.

'I love your smile. I've been awake ages.'

I felt her hand glide down my side. It wasn't my hand she was shaking.

'I'd have let you sleep, but I'm flying out...'

I must have looked blank.

'Surely you remember?'

'I remember everything,' I lied. I remembered nothing. How much had I drunk last night? I could feel her manoeuvring for a kiss.

'Give me a minute, gorgeous. My breath must smell like an Irish wake.'

I got up, naked, noticed her uniform carefully laid out on the second queen size bed, and two used condoms close to the bin but not in. I grabbed the open can of full-fat Coke – the black doctor! – from the dressing table and headed straight to the bathroom, where I downed it in one and gave my teeth a quick brush.

My word association memory was flashing up a picture of Jeeves. Butler, her name was Butler. And the T was Tricia. Tricia Butler. It was all coming back. She was from Woking, a classically trained cellist who had been an air stewardess for ten years. A beautiful one at that, and pretty kinky too, if memory served. They didn't teach her style of hand and finger vibrato at the Royal Academy of Music.

I grinned. Yeah, now I remembered everything.

There had been a little ag on the flight in business class. A few ICF lads were getting lairy, nothing more than sozzled argy-bargy, but they looked menacing and I'd calmed them down. Trish was impressed. She had the night off. And, as Andre Schweitzer was out on a job, we hit the town and proceeded to get more hammered than an antique blacksmith's anvil.

Well, I did at least. Trish looked a lot healthier than I felt. She positively glowed.

''Urry up on 'Arry,' she half-sung at me, presumably in case I had missed it the first time. 'Come on gorgeous! Time and air traffic control wait for no man or woman.'

I came out smiling and got back into bed. She ran her fingers over my stomach.

'How did you get these abs?'

'I box a bit.' Man and boy, as it happened.

'Fab abs…' – her fingers worked their way down – 'rad nads…and ooh look, little Harry is up for grabs.'

He certainly was. United Airlines had a slogan, 'Fly the friendly skies', but I was far keener on flying BA Tricia's friendly thighs once more before she left. It's not every week you have free time in Manhattan.

In the event, we managed it twice before she had to take off. I still had it.

***

The digital clock on the bedstand said 6.39am, only now I was alone. The only reminder of the Tricia Butler was the lingering smell of her $60 perfume. That and the scattering of condoms. They were Yank ones, Trojan – presumably designed to appeal to blokes who liked to think they were hung like a horse.

Remnants of cocaine littered the side table like a light scattering of dandruff. Yeah. She'd brought two grams through customs and we'd consumed the lot like greedy rock stars, washed down with dark spiced rum. There were a couple of orange pills too – Adderrall, a gift, in case I felt the need for speed. She used it regularly, she'd said, to keep her up on the long-haul flights.

On the floor was the paperback I'd started reading on the flight over, Slow Horses by Mick Herron.

To think the only off-duty recreation I was expecting this trip was to finish it…

I pushed my breakfast tray to one side, scooped up the Johnnies, walked over to the far wall, and skimmed them at the bin. Three on target, one bounced off the rim. I smiled. Something didn't feel right, though. Not medically, mentally. It took a moment to figure it out because it wasn't a feeling I was used to.

It was guilt.

Yeah, Harry Tyler, once the Metropolitan Police's greatest player, was having a twinge of conscious. Ever since I moved in with Amanda, I had promised myself I would jack in other birds. Mandy made me happy, and I didn't want to fuck that up again.

Shit on a shitty stick.

I'd call her later and lie convincingly.

That was one of the problems with my old job. Lying became second nature. It was as easy as breathing. I am working hard on being a better man. Or is that just a lie I tell myself?

The memories of my failed marriages hung over me like an urban smog. All that micro-aggression. And of course, all of my admittedly major transgressions. Sometimes the thrill of casual temptation with nano-emotion and zero commitment is hard to resist.

I scooped the blonde hairs up from the pillow absent-mindedly and binned them too, like I was hiding the evidence from a vigilant girlfriend or an imaginary forensics team. Soon sunshine would be pouring through the hotel window. I opened the curtains, trying to take it all in. This was my first morning on my first trip to the Big Apple, and the streets were already bustling.

Suddenly Stevie Wonder was in my head. *New York, New York. Just like I'd pictured it, skyscrapers and everything...*

The all-night deli over the road was as busy now as it had been at 1am. I felt like a kid from an inner London council estate on his first day at a safari park. What a trip this was going to be!

It was also the easiest £10K I had ever made, and it came with a first-class airline ticket both ways and a six-night, all-expenses-paid stay at the Park Hyatt – one of New York's swankiest hotels. I had been looking forward to the concierge looking down his upturned schnoz at me, and I hadn't been disappointed. Obsequious to other guests, the bloke had glared at me when I got here yesterday afternoon like I was something he'd stepped in at a rodeo.

It was the kind of look that said he knew I was completely the wrong class of person for their puffed-up, over-priced, la-di-da gaff and, also, that he knew there was fuck-all squared he could do about it.

My real name is Harry Dean, but my passport still said Tyler – the name of my favourite 'legend', the fancy label given to the character undercover cops operate under. Or should I say ex-undercover-cop, as well as ex-public enemy and now a fully qualified private eye. Almost respectable.

I suppose I should also mention a double ex-husband and a pretty shitty father.

Even though New York was new to me, everything about the city felt familiar – the yellow taxis, red fire hydrants, blue post boxes, the steam coming out of the ground... I'd grown up pouring over Marvel and DC comics; I had gobbled up TV shows like Kojak, Taxi, Law & Order and NYPD Blue – though nothing topped Seinfeld and The Sopranos – so the 45-minute limo ride into Manhattan from JFK had felt like a trip down memory lane. I was ticking off sites I'd seen in the movies – Queens, the Midtown Tunnel. Did I mention they sent a limo? Let me mention it again. A black Chrysler Executive driven by Tommy Byrne, a widowed ex-cop from the Bronx. Two daughters, four grandchildren, and a life-long devotion to the Mets.

I had him drive me past Radio City Music Hall, Central Park and Tom's Restaurant (also known as Monk's Café on Seinfeld) on Broadway and West 112 Street – just in case I didn't have time to get there later in the week. Then I signed for an hour's non-existent waiting time and bunged him two 'lobsters' – 40bucks – for his trouble.

The job was a good'un. I had seven full days to try to hunt down Amelia Storey of the Virginia Water Storeys, no less. The 21-year-old heiress had walked straight out of the London School of Economics and legged it to the capital of the world. Her worried father, the Right Hon Sir Timothy Storey, told me she had been 'radicalised' at college and he was concerned that she may have been converted by a mind control cult keen to get their hands on the millions in her trust fund, not to mention the millions more coming her way when Timmy baby and the fragrant Lady Gabriella peg it.

The way they told it, sweet respectable Amelia had fallen in with some low-rent, lentil-chomping, soap-dodging anarchist punks, dropped out of college, cleared out her savings and high-tailed it here, to the five boroughs with an undesirable half-Yank guitarist and Class War activist who called himself Jason Hate. Yeah. What better way to screw the upper classes than by literally fucking Lady Muck?

This is where Andre Schweitzer came into play. I'd first met him when he was an NYPD detective and I was still one of the Met's best undercover operators – or at least one of the luckiest. He was a shrewd investigator, open to lateral thinking, with a keen interest in the Lower East Side's punk underground. And as I knew from seeing him in action, he was a hard man to kill.

I had helped him nab a nasty bag of worms and sweep the scumbag back to Septic Land without any legal authority to do so. It was what the Yanks call a deniable operation. Now it was payback time. To find that runaway heiress I was going to need his lifetime of local knowledge and New York street nous.

My ten large fee had been paid in advance, fully and irrespective of results, plus I had anything-goes expenses. Not that I wouldn't do my damnedest to find the missing minx.

I was due to meet Andre in Murray's Bagels at 8.30am, still over an hour away. I looked at the remnants of my $30 room service breakfast – eggs benedict with salmon, plus juice and black coffee. I could eat that again, I thought, and already I knew I would. Cheers Sir Tim. Happy days!

Chapter 3

By my reckoning, Murray's gaff was a 40-minute walk away, so I decided to take a slow saunter down Sixth Avenue and soak up some of the sights. The Avenue of the Americas, as New Yorkers don't call it, is nearly four miles of uptown traffic and familiar architecture, passing through the Flatiron District, SoHo, Greenwich Village and more. The Empire State Building was even more imposing from a pedestrian's point of view.

I reached West 14th Street and realised the bagel emporium was less than a moon shot away (I knew my baseball). Waiting to cross, I caught a glimpse of a dark blue Chrysler sedan parked to my left. There are a thousand dark blue Chryslers in Manhattan, but this one was different. It had two stickers on its back window that made it stand out. One said New Jersey Devils, and the lower one said Twisted Sister: SMF. Sick Mother Fuckers! That took me back. Dee Snider! 'We're not gonna take it…' Populism welded to angry, hard-hitting blue-collar rock. What a band. What a sound. And what a look! Twisted Sister were half dockers in drag and half Halloween coming early and never leaving. An ideal booking for bah mitzvahs and children's parties.

I crossed the street and spotted my destination straight away. It was 8.20am and Andre was already there. I strolled in and found him chomping on a Belly Lox sandwich.

'Hey, H!' he shouted, standing up and pumping my hand with a big grin. 'Good to see ya, buddy.'

'You too mate.'

Andre was shorter than me, but stockier. He wore a green flight jacket, with badges – he'd call them pins – spelling out his allegiance to the New York Giants,

Agnostic Front and S.H.A.R.P., whatever the fuck that was.

'I'm guessing you've eaten.'

'Yeah, two hours ago.'

'And that was two hours after you'd woken up, right?'

'Right.'

'And you're here for seven days, so by the time you get on New York hours…'

'It'll be time to fly home.'

'Unless you hook up with one of our fine waitresses and turn it into a proper vacation.'

He nodded at the elderly lady who was busy taking orders and added, 'Maybe not Bessie.'

'Maybe nobody, mate. I'm loved up.'

I decided against mentioning Tricia.

'Tell all.'

What was to tell? I'd been shacked up with Mandy for two months now; it was my first real relationship since the second divorce, and it was a proper love job, hearts and flowers, dopamine, oxytocin, and norepinephrine flowing… All that old cobblers.

'She's the one, mate.'

Andre feigned surprise, clutching his chest in mock shock.

'Until the next one.'

'Cynic.'

'Realist. You want a drink?'

'Yeah. Black filter coffee. Nothing fancy.'

'Because…'

'Because I'm a regular Joe...'

'And you like your Joe regular.'

We both laughed. It was a classic Marty Crane quote and we shared a mutual and abiding love of *Frasier*.

Bessie took my order.

'So, what's the job, bruv?'

I briefly sketched out the situation and pulled out a fairly recent picture of Amelia Storey. The torn Exploited t-shirt and the grubby leather jacket disguised her inherent poshness but couldn't dampen her natural beauty.

Andre sat up. 'I know her,' he said with absolute conviction. Bingo!

'You sure?'

'Yeah, she lives in a crusty anarchist squat down on the Lower East Side. I've seen her on demos. She volunteers at a homeless shelter and hangs out at punk clubs. Lives with Tippy Jay. I know that cos when I saw them together, I thought how the hell did that cheap drugged-up ass-hole midget get that lucky!?!'

I thought for a moment. 'Tippy Jay, is that short for Jason?'

'He's short for genetic reasons, but yeah, seems likely.'

He looked at the picture again. 'She sure stands out in a crowd. And you say her folks are loaded?'

'Yeah. Fort Knox minted. So, Lower East Side. Not too far?'

'Two-mile walk, tops.'

'Can you point me in the right direction?'

'I can do better than that, pardner. I can come with you. But I might need your help with something too, if you've got time.'

I gave a no-problem shrug. He ordered two coffees to go, and we set off.

'How was the flight over?'

'I had a bit of excitement.'

'Yeah?'

'A few ICF boys were playing up in business class, so I strolled back from the posh end with a bottle of Heidsieck, non-vintage, dropped a few names, cracked some jokes about Billy Gayle and some of the old Mile End mob and calmed them down. Granted, the zolpidem I'd sprinkled in their bubbly might have helped.'

Andre laughed.

'You are West Ham though, aren't you?'

'Solidly mate, irons for life, but I don't really know the faces other than by sight and reputation. Luckily, I had a u/c mate, Irish Kev, imbedded in Swallow's firm for a year or two, who used to use me as a sounding board.'

Andre nodded. 'Tough gig.'

'I'll say. The guy before him wasn't so lucky. He came out the Boleyn one Saturday and some plank in uniform shouted 'Oi Steve, how are ya?' at the top of his voice.'

'Blowing it for him?'

'Faster than Linda Lovelace on piece rate.'

'Voice is ''Obson's' right?'

'You got it.'

Andre had become obsessed with Cockney slang when we first worked together.

'Hey, was Cass Pennant on the plane?'

'Nah.'

'Shame I'd like to meet him. I read his book. Interesting guy.'

'I'll get him over. Mutual friends. You still put on speaking events, don't you? Cass will come if there's a few simoleons in it. He's what we call a proper ducker and diver, an Arfur Daley.'

'Like Bilko?'

'Yeah, just like your Sgt Bilko or our Del-Boy. I'll get you one of his fire-damaged woks.'

'Fire-damaged woks?'

'If you fancy one. He does a nice line in rain-damaged brollies and underwater hair-dryers too. What d'you think?'

'I'm thinking a week with you could easily feel like a month.'

'You love me really.'

'Define love.'

We stopped at the corner of East 2nd Street and Bowery and I clocked another dark blue Chrysler sedan pass us, identical to the one I'd spotted up by Murray's

Bagels, even down to the stickers plastered across the back window – the New Jersey Devils and Twisted Sister: SMF.

'Have you got a mate who can trace a licence plate?'

'Sure, for a few bucks. Why?'

'I keep seeing the same car. It could be a coincidence, or it could be we're under surveillance from the world's thickest feds.'

'How so?'

'What should be an unmarked dark blue Chrysler sedan has got a Devil's ice hockey sticker in its back window, along with one saying Twisted Sister: SMF.'

'Sick Mother Fuckers?'

'The same.'

'That's not the Feds. And even the NYPD ain't that dumb.' He thought for a moment. 'Maybe something murkier out of Newark.'

'If it's Tony Soprano, it'll make my year.'

'The real Jersey boys aren't that smart. What's the plate?'

'UH8 MES'.

He nodded. 'Got it. Let me know if you see it again.'

'Will do. You still with Stephanie, the publishing bird?'

'Solid as a rock. Why, you thinking of doing your memoir?'

'Yeah, good call. Everything I ever did, every dirty trick, every dirtier bird, and every clever con… 99.9per cent redacted.'

He laughed. We crossed another road. No Chrysler sedan.

'What did you want to ask me about?'

'Call it another coincidence but it involves a prominent Italian-American 'businessman'. I'll fill you in after we meet Amelia. We're nearly there.'

***

'There' was an old warehouse converted into a shelter with a 24/7 soup kitchen for the homeless. The walls were blitzed with posters bearing radical anarchist slogans that screamed 'Libertat!' and 'No Gods, No Masters'. Old, black and white stencilled ones from English punk bands Crass and Conflict stood out compared to cosier domestic ones like the rather staid 'There's Nothing More Punk Rock Than Mutual Aid'.

How the hell did that fit in with Lydon screaming 'I wanna destroy the passer-by'? I wondered.

A smell hung in the air; last night's smoke haunting the hall like a mellow Ganja mist, reluctant to leave.

There were a few women scattered about. Most were badly dressed stark raving crazy tree-shaggers who looked like they'd wandered in from a Friends of the Vegan Trustafarian Cyclist & Carrot-Crunching Club student demo. One, a bit punkier, was serving soup by the ladle to a young thin-faced guy who could easily have been on an all-you-can-smoke crystal meth diet since Christmas. But when she turned in our direction, it wasn't Amelia.

I looked at Andre and shook my head.

'Give me a minute,' he said.

He went off and spoke to a tall woman with a kind face and an unkind cardigan who directed him to the kitchen. He was in and out quickly.

'The rota says your girl is due to be on soup duty in five minutes. Let's wait.'

I nodded. It was chilled enough here, and if hunger kicked in, the soup was free. Twelve minutes later Amelia Storey ambled in with a couple of pals. Her hair was different. It looked like a rats' nest dipped in a rainbow but there was no mistaking the cheekbones.

'That's her, standing under the poster that says Make Art, Not War. Hair like an action painting. Next to the scruffy kid and the butch bird with the feather cut.'

'Got her. Yeah, that's Tippy Jay. The butch broad is Sammy something, I think. Let me speak to them first.'

Schweitzer walked over. Tippy's face lit up. 'Comrade,' he said loudly, pumping his hand. It was a good sign. As Andre spoke, all three of them looked over at me. Amelia's face dropped, but she nodded her head. Tippy called another volunteer over to man the stand and three of them walked over, leaving the tougher woman standing watching.

I smiled and offered Amelia my hand. She hesitated but only briefly before shaking it. The smell of skunk hung around her like a cloak. There was something else that hung around her too, a casually provocative sensuality that even black jeans and a Rancid 'And Out Come The Wolves' t-shirt couldn't mask.

'No offence, mister, but let's make this quick.' Her accent was more American than I'd expected, mid-Atlantic with a New York edge, but she was even more beautiful in the flesh than she was in her photo. The metal badge on her jacket was a red clenched fist. Very rad...

'Thanks, can I call you Amelia?'

'Sure, mister...?'

'Harry. Harry Tyler. Call me Harry.'

'We'll get coffees,' said Jay. 'How do you like it?'

'Thanks. Like La Toya, sweet and black.'

I turned back to Amelia, whose arms were folded defensively across a bosom that lesser men than me would cheerfully describe as ample. Her face was fashion model perfect.

'You're doing a good job here.'

She nodded; her baby blue eyes still stone cold.

'These posters, very radical.'

She sighed. 'When I feed the poor, they call me a saint, when I ask why they've got no food, they call me a Communist.'

I nodded. 'Helder Camara.' I'd infiltrated an anarchist group back home in the dim and distant.

She looked at me, surprised, and smiled. The ice was broken. I seized the advantage.

'I'm not going to hassle you, Amelia. Your old man was worried about your safety and asked me to track you down. My job was to find you, make sure that you're okay and report back. That's it.'

'As you can see Mr Tyler… Harry, I'm perfectly fine.' The diction was now more Home Counties England.

The butch woman with the feather cut hair came over and stood by her like a protective mother hen.

'Everything okay, Amelia?' she asked.

'All cool, Sammy.'

Butch shot me a look that could have curdled the soup and walked off. She was about 5ft 10 and powerfully built, and her hair was unusual, old school skinhead girl from the front, and a Number two razor cut at the back. Despite her obvious displeasure at my presence, she was a handsome woman with a strong jaw line. I smiled at Amelia and carried on.

'And you aren't being coerced to stay here?'

'On the contrary, I feel liberated for the first time in my entire life. I trust Andre, he's one of us, and he says I can trust you. So here goes. I needed space, Mr Tyler. I needed to get away from my father. The man is so controlling he makes Hitler's Schutzstaffel look like the Care Bears. If he could follow me with drones every waking hour, he would. It's suffocating. He wanted to marry me off to some dull carpet millionaire from Gravesend and knock out a platoon of grand kids.'

'So, you escaped?'

'I ran for me fucking life, mate,' she said breaking into a Cockney accent worthy of Dick Van Dyke. 'Jay might not be Donald Trump but he's lovely and respectful and he really cares about other people.'

I nodded. I was pretty good at reading people having spent years around psychopaths, villains, conmen, and thieves. I knew all the liar's tells – the chin touching, the mouth covering, the head movements – and Amelia was displaying none of them. I felt she was telling the truth. Or at least that she believed what she was saying.

'I wanted to live a little, Harry. I've had a very privileged life up until new. I decided to have a purposeful one instead and to help people worse off than me.'

She looked at me like she was weighing me up.

'There's something else...' She hesitated.

'Go on.'

'Between us?'

'Pinky promise.'

'My dear darling daddy did things to me growing up that no girl should ever have to suffer. Even Jay doesn't know. He, he...'

Jay and Andre walked back with the coffees in polythene cups. She stopped dead.

'I'll tell you another time, maybe. And if I do, you will understand why I prefer to keep an ocean between me and the oh-so respectable Right Honourable arsehole Sir Timothy Storey.'

'Of course.' That rang true too.

'So send mummy and daddy my undying love and tell them I need for nothing. Tell them I'm enjoying a life of meaning, helping the poor and underprivileged, tell them I'll come back for Christmas next year but please emphasise this – if they attempt to get in touch before that I will go off the radar so fast and so deep even our mutual pal Mr Schweitzer won't be able to find me.'

'I'll do that.'

'Thank you. Maybe someday I will have had enough of it and I'll decide to go back to the Home Counties and bang a provincial carpet magnate on his soft plush shag-pile but it'll be on my terms, not Daddy's.'

She laughed and added. 'Or alternatively you could tell him you found me dead and buried in the same landfill they dumped the Lehman Brothers… which would probably make him just as happy.'

I smiled.

'No, just tell him that you found me, I'm well, I've found someone who makes me happy, and I'll be back when I'm good and ready.'

'Can I take a picture to prove it?'

'Crack away.'

I took a small Polaroid camera out of my jacket.

'Hang on,' she walked over to a table and picked up a newspaper. 'Take it of me holding today's New York Post, like you would in a hostage situation.'

She laughed again and so did I. I took a couple of shots and said I'd email the news and the photo over this evening so he'd see it tomorrow.

'Or you could keep him hanging. I don't want him to think I was so easy to find. Oh, but hold on, that would negate the point of the Poloroids wouldn't it? No matter. I doubt that he'll be on the next plane over.'

The pictures came out well. Even in her dressed-down trampy schmutta she looked good enough to be on the cover of Vogue.

'We done?' asked Andre.

'Sorted,' I replied.

'*Saullll-ted*,' he mocked. 'Come on, let's get you back to Mary Poppins.'

'Are you East End, Harry?' asked Amelia.

'Not far off.'

She kissed my cheek. 'Safe trip home.'

Outside, I shook Andre by the hand. 'Cheers pal.'

'No problem.'

The door slammed shut behind us with a clatter. I couldn't believe how easy that had been. I had to treat this man to something more than a street vendor hot dog. I trusted his judgement more than I would the hotel concierge's.

'I've been thinking, if you could eat anywhere in town and money weren't an issue, where would it be?'

'Ah, maybe the Armani, on Fifth. Out of my blue-collar price range but it gets great reviews.'

I looked at my snide Tissot T-sport. 12.44. 'I'll see you there at 7. On me. You're right, I owe you dinner.'

'Hey H, I was kidding. You don't have to do that, man. You've helped me enough.'

'Don't worry about it, it's on Sir Tim really.'

'What he's like?'

'Posh, privileged, pompous, entitled… Looks like the Pillsbury Doughboy. Polite but probably over-bearing and controlling to subordinates. A tyrant to his family, obsequious to his betters I'd imagine, but to his peer group, no problem at all.'

'So no different to any other jerk in the suburban members' only golf-club?'

'Yep. That's pretty much my take.'

'What a geezer.'

What a creep more like.

***

As we made our way back on foot, I noticed a beaten-up yellow Volkswagen campervan behind us, then in front of us, and then behind us again. I would have thought nothing more of it if I hadn't also seen it again driving past the Park Hyatt when I got back.

Chapter 4

Back at the hotel, I studied the two photographs – the one I had brought with me and the Polaroid I had just taken. Hairstyle aside they were identical except for one small thing. Amelia's eyes looked paler in the original photo. But that didn't concern me. It was down to the l lighting or flash photography. In every other aspect the two pictures were clearly the same person. I used the hotel business centre to scan the Polaroid and email it to Sir Tim, then I set the alarm for 6pm and hit the sack.

I came to just before it went off and took a long shower savouring the power of the five-star hotel deluge. I ironed a crisp white blue Ralph Lauren shirt and fresh black Polo Ralph Lauren jeans, topping off the look with classic Belmont black brogues and a black Stone Island jacket – I don't normally mix brands but the Septics have about as much clue about fashion as Kanye West has about keeping his thoughts to himself.

It was a warm evening, so I took a slow walk to Fifth Avenue taking in the mid-town sights and the bustling crowds, looking for danger that never came. No dark blue Chrysler sedans were out cruising – maybe the Jersey mob worked office hours. No funny-looking hippie campervans either.

The Armani Italian restaurant was inside the Armani store. Not too surprising. There was a private elevator that took you up from the street, but I opted to go in and walk up a winding white ramp that twisted up, passing two floors of over-priced gowns and fancy leather goods. Andre was already there, his green flight jacket over the back of his chair and his first bottle of lager on the go.

He was squinting at the menu like he was Mr Magoo and it was the bottom line of an optician's eye chart.

The fidgety waiter didn't look too sure of him.

'Any good?' I asked.

'About 35bucks a main. Upper East Side prices. Fuck, eleven bucks for sparkling water. Aqua Armani…'

I sat down and grinned. A less nervy sommelier handed me the wine list. I scanned down to the southern Italian whites.

'The Sicilian Grillo is very good,' he said conspiratorially.

I looked. $39. 'We'll take that. You want another beer too, mate?'

'Wine is fine,' Andre said, muttering 'but whisky's quicker' under his breath.

The food waiter was impatiently transferring his weight from one foot to another like a small child desperate for a piddle. We took pity and ordered. I went for seared sea scallops with potato gratin, Andre had the bone-in veal chop Milanese.

'So that went well today…'

'It couldn't have gone better. Almost too good to be true.'

'Don't jinx it. Man, that broad's a looker.'

'She's trouble mate. Trouble waiting to happen.'

'How so? Did something go wrong?'

'No, no. I meant any bird that stunning is going to cause trouble whether she means to or not. And when a woman's beautiful and brainy and full of the confidence that only the English public school system or Al-Qaeda can instil in you, then trouble is *gonna come* like a hard rain in a Bob Dylan song. Amelia Storey is the sort of women knights fought dragons for.'

'You ain't kidding.'

He took a slug of his over-priced beer.

'I might have another…'

'Be my guest.'

'So what ya going to do with your few days on paid holiday, H?'

'I used to love NYPD Blue, so thought I'd maybe check out a few filming locations. Y'know, Little Italy and Chinatown, all around lower east Manhattan. Alphabet City.'

'Did you ever watch Kojak?'

'Of course! Who didn't! *Who loves ya baby?*'

'They shot scenes for that all over too, the Empire Diner, Bethesda Terrace, Chelsea Piers. I'll write a few down.'

'Cheers.'

'Another great show...'

'Kojak! *Hug the wall like it's your mother...* They should remake that.'

'I could play Theo. I've got the accent for it.'

'You've got the haircut for it too.'

The Sommelier came back with the plonk. I waved away his attempt to get me to taste it.

'Just pour, my friend. And let it flow.'

I waited until he walked away and lowered my voice.

'So tell me about the job you want help with?'

'It's not so much a job as an unsolvable crime.'

I sat up. Intrigued. 'Go on.'

'Have you heard of Giovanni Infantino?'

I shook my head. 'Should I have?'

Andre glanced around to check that no waiters were hovering and lowered his voice to little more than a whisper.

'He's known in crime circles as Johnny Baby. A respectable Italian-American businessman who everyone knows is, or at least was, an underboss in the Bonanno family before his apparent retirement. I know he's still pulling strings because the boss can barely tie his own shoelaces. Anyhow, Johnny had a place in Vinegar Hill but last year he bought a pad in Central Park South for more money than the likes of you and me will earn in a lifetime. And he had one of those hidden rooms fitted where he kept his wife's furs and jewellery, his frigging jewellery, a few over-priced antiques and his two prize possessions, Bob Dylan's handwritten and autographed lyrics to Joey, and a Matisse painting, La Pasterale that was pinched from Paris four years ago, worth maybe $18million. Any-who, he has some kind of a gathering for his Mafia mates and groupies and associated businessmen the weekend before last and a few of the guys get to check out his special room. One at a time. To cut a long story short, one of them appears to have replaced Dylan's lyrics and the Matisse with forgeries. The real ones have vanished but nobody knows how. Johnny had one of those airport x-ray machines set up and a capo on the door searching people on the way out – a fucking tough cookie called Giuliano Clarini. There's no way anyone goes in or comes out with anything with Giulo around. They call him La Cosa.'

I thought for a moment. 'The Thing?'

'*Precisamente.* That's what his friends call him anyway. His enemies prefer a more explanatory English nickname Satan's Pitbull.'

I grunted. 'That Dylan song, Joey, it was about Joey Gallo, wasn't it?'

'It was. Crazy Joe, caporegime of the Colombo crime family. Gunned down in a clam house in Little Italy, called Umbertos. Murder still unsolved…'

'How dangerous would you say Johnny Baby is?'

'There's a saying in the Village – you don't step on Superman's cape, you don't spit into the wind, you don't pull the mask off the Green Goblin and you don't mess around with Giovanni Infantino.'

'And yet somebody is…'

'Somebody with a death wish.'

I sipped the wine. Tasted great. 'Are the Mob still a big thing here? I thought the Feds nicked more than a 100 of them a couple of years ago.'

'They did. 2011. It was the biggest bust in FBI history. The got the boss of the Colombo family too. And you know what? It didn't mean jack… The five families are still intact. They're still connected. And they're growing. Organised crime is getting more organised, not less. My friends in low places tell me that they have been busy forging links with the Mexican and Colombian drug cartels, and the Ndrangheta from the old country.'

I nodded. I knew about them. A nasty mob out of the mountains of Calabria, as hard as 2 Para as just as disciplined.

'A proper firm. They've been around for centuries,' I said, almost to myself.

'They've got a bigger network than the friggin' internet. We're talking about a serious growth. The Feds haven't even dented them.'

I downed the wine, and chummy boy was back to fill me before the glass hit the table.

'Bad times for the good guys.'

'Even the good guys are compromised. They've got goons in the NYPD. A couple high up is the word.'

I shook my head. 'Fuck all we can do about it. But I would like to have a crack at your closed-room mystery before I go. To solve the unsolvable crime…'

And size up the guy, I thought to myself.

'Is there any way you can get me in there?'

'Sure. I'll call Johnny Baby and fix up a visit. Are you going to feel like going down there midmorning tomorrow? I've got a surveillance thing in the early afternoon.'

'Mate, I'll be ready to roll at 6am.'

We talked about music for a bit. He told me to check out a couple of bands I hadn't heard of, Agnostic Front from the Lower East Side and Social Distortion from California. I mentioned the King Blues, Missing Andy from Essex and Londoners Buster Shuffle who I likened to Madness blended with a large dollop of Chas & Dave.

My nosh came out first, the scallops served with short stacks of potato gratin. Then his veal chop. The crust on it looked so heavenly I nearly sent back the scallops.

'The first time I heard about this place it was when Donald Trump got pictured here in the New York Post.'

'Trump? Amelia mentioned him. He's The Apprentice guy on TV over here, isn't he?'

'Among other things. Real estate and self-publicity mainly. He's involved with Miss Universe. He used Mob-run labour to build his Trump Tower which is just a walk away from here. Word is his old man was tied up with them. Check it out if you have time. It looks pretty cool. It has a kind of jagged façade. Check out his missus too, whose façade is definitely not jagged. She's hot, H. 'Otter than a deep-fried otter, as you'd probably say.'

I smiled weakly. The jet-lag was kicking in.

'Now he runs with bigger bandits. He reckons he's pals with Putin, the creepy Russian putz who's allergic to shirts, and Aras Agalarov, a property billionaire. I heard Trump on TV, he's a big Putin fan-boy. I saw somewhere that the Russians paid him a fortune to stage a pageant over there.'

I stifled a yawn.

'Am I that boring?'

'Mate, it's the jet-lag.'

'Call it circadian dysrhythmia, it sounds like a medical condition. You'll get more sympathy.'

'Circadian Dysrhythmia, didn't he marry one of the Kardashians?'

'Almost certainly. Lasted three months and they made ten million bucks from flogging the divorce exclusive to the supermarket rags.'

I grinned. 'Mate, you know how it is, I'm gonna have to shoot.' I pulled out two hundred-dollar notes. 'This will cover it, have more if you want, mate, just get me a receipt so I can bill it to Lord Moneybags.'

'Will do mate. I'll toast your memory with a large Vecchia Romagna.'

'That another mob guy?'

'You've still got it.'

'Well mind you don't catch it.'

We both stood up, and I shook his hand. 'Let me know about tomorrow.'

'I'll meet you in the lobby at 10am. I reckon it'll be on, but if not I'll take you someplace else. You can't do the big bad apple without a tour guide.'

Almost exactly one mile from the Armani, in East 67th Street, Captain Buster Campbell sighed audibly as he sat down at his office desk. If he hadn't realised that involuntary grunts and groans were a by-product of age, one glance at the reflection of his weathered face in his hipflask was enough to remind him he was five weeks away from his 63rd birthday – the NYPD's mandatory retirement age. That and the constant aches and pains in his thigh, knees, heels, and lower back.

He poured himself half a mug of Bushmills and breathed out, sounding for all the world like a slowly deflating paddling pool. At least he'd made it to the end. Most of his fellow rookies from the start had either dropped out, dropped dead, or retired early from injuries.

Buster opened the top right-hand drawer of his desk looking for his Hershey bar and caught a whiff of decomposition. There was a dead pigeon lying on top of a pile of documents where the chocolate ought to be. Some sicko had even taken the time to fashion a small noose around its neck with some thick string.

Motherfuckers!

Buster clenched his fists and bared his teeth for as long as it took him to count to ten. They'd done this. The bad apples. This was their subtle-as-cyanide way of sending him a message, bad cops to honest cop, snitches get stitches. Except the metaphor didn't work too well. A stool pigeon was a criminal informant, not a police officer who sniffed out bent cops. His thick-as-mince tormentors, and he had a pretty good idea who they were, were unlikely to understand the difference.

He breathed deeply and looked at the helpless bird again. Its plump body, now lifeless and useless, lay rigid in a small sea of its own fallen feathers. It was useless and unwanted, completely beyond salvation, it stank to high heaven and it would attract vermin... it was actually a better metaphor for a growing breed of New York cops – the dirty, grubby ones.

How many bent cops does it take to save a pigeon? None, they won't save a pigeon, they just beat it to death in the back room for being black and blue...

Buster smiled wearily. Fists un-gripped and teeth unclenched, he calmly deposited the feathery corpse in the nearest trash can and closed the desk drawer softly. Then he stopped grinning. He took his mug and poured the remaining whiskey in Rosie Maloney's flowerpot. This situation demanded a degree caution, concentration and, above all, clarity. The dead bird wasn't a refugee from a Monty Python sketch. It was a serious threat and very definitely one that should be logged and reported to I.A. But to hell with that. Buster Campbell would deal with this himself. He would hunt down the enemy and tear out their cold, poisonous hearts with his bare hands.

Figuratively. Of course?

Figuratively, maybe.

Chapter 5
Tuesday, May 13th

I woke up at 5.45am. An improvement and ate the same room service breakfast. Groundhog Day never tasted better. Then I took a slow stroll around the neighbourhood until the business centre opened at 9am. There were no chalk outlines. And no sedan tail either. Tsk. New York was slipping. I made one big decision though – tomorrow I would skip the hotel breakfast and go for a hot knish from a street stand. Plus, I still had to sample an authentic "dirty water dog" – what the locals call a $1 hot dog from a cart, with mustard, tomato sauce and grilled onions. The '*woiks*'.

By 8.59am I was back in the Park Hyatt, still annoying the concierge just by breathing. I headed to the business centre to pick up a couple of newspapers and check my emails. There were a couple from Mandy, a job enquiry I'd get back to next week, more spam than a war-time larder, and a rather odd message from Sir Timothey Storey. He was grateful for my news and appreciated me taking a picture of Amelia but for some reason he now wanted me to get a video message from her – and get it to him by end of play today. Use the limo service to get about town, he'd added, it's what they've been paid for.

'Wasn't the picture enough?' said Andre when he rocked up at 10am.

'Apparently not. Can we get to her again?'

'I'll phone Tippy later on, he won't be up yet.'

'I took the liberty of alerting Tommy Byrne, my all-hours chauffeur. He'll drive us to Infantino's place and wait to drive us on to wherever Amelia wants to meet.'

Andre sighed. 'There was one bit of bad news, sorry H, Johnny Baby wants to meet tomorrow morning instead of today. Something's come up. Can you meet me at my office at 10am tomorrow and we'll go from there?'

He handed me a dog-eared card with an address in Hell's Kitchen.

'Right at the heart of Gotham, eh?'

'Yeah. And you're Robin. You'll see inside the Batcave tomorrow, 10 sharp. And I'll ring you after I speak to Tippy.'

**

Andre got hold of Tippy on this fourth attempt and we were set. Three hours later Tommy dropped me back at the soup kitchen to meet Amelia.

'Shall I wait, Mr Tyler?' he asked in his warm, understated way.

'Thanks Tommy. Yes please. Hopefully this will be quick.'

**

The smell of dope hit me as soon as I walked in the door. Much stronger than yesterday. You would get higher than a motorised kite just from breathing the fumes. Andre was already inside, with Tippy Jay and Amelia who looked seriously pissed off.

'He's playing games with you, Harry, the sick fuck,' she said bluntly.

'And nice to see you again too.'

She smiled briefly. Amelia looked hot even in jeans and a Social Distortion t-shirt.

'I'm doing this for you not him, but let's make it quick please, I've got soup to serve.'

Andre whisked out his iPhone 5 which made mine look as up to date as your granny's old rotary dial house phone.

'Ready when you are, kiddo,' he said.

Amelia sat on a table and looked straight into his device.

'Go,' he said.

'Hello Daddio, this is your loving daughter live, broadcasting to you from somewhere in New York City. As you can see, I am very much me. I'm also very much alive. I'm well and I'm happy but be advised that if you ever send Mr Tyler back to pester me any more – and I do mean ever – I'll make sure that neither you nor he will ever find me again. That's it. You know what we want. Over to you. Love to mother. See you when I see you.'

Job done.

Amelia pulled me to one side. 'A word in private please, Mr Tyler.'

'Sure.'

She steered me into a corner. From a distance it probably looked like she was shaking my hand but she was actually passing me a USB stick.

'This will explain everything, Harry,' she said. Her voice was soft and husky; her tone almost pleading. 'There's a lot on it and it's dynamite, so keep it safe, and I mean really safe. Don't keep it on your person, don't leave it in your hotel room. I am not paranoid. Believe me. All will become clear.'

'Got it.'

She kissed me on the cheek and headed for the soup queue. Well, I'd got what I came for, but what did she mean by saying 'You know what we want'? It was a puzzling phrase. I walked back and shook hands with Tippy and Andre, then I walked out and asked good old Tommy Byrne to take me back to the hotel.

'Have you got any plans tonight, sir?' he asked.

'I was thinking of watching old episodes of Star Trek: The Next Generation until I crash out.'

'Well that's one plan. But here's another. How about you come back to mine for a proper family meal either tonight or another night this week if you have the time? A few whiskies, some chat, authentic home-cooked nosh.'

'That's very kind of you Tommy but…'

'No buts, you've treated me well. I would like to repay you.'

'There's no need, but thank you.'

I thought it through. 'Is Thursday okay with you? I figure I'll be less cream-cracker'd and more on top of things by then.'

'Cream-cracker'd?'

'Sorry. Knackered. Or as you'd say, bushed.'

'Tuckered out!'

'Exactly that. I really appreciate your offer, Tommy and I don't want to fall akip on your dining table. I'm not one to look a gift horse in the mouth.'

'I can't promise horse but my girl is a dab hand with mutton and beef…'

I laughed and so did he. A good man.

When I got back to the Hyatt, I put the USB stick in a hotel envelope and had reception lock it up for me in their safe. Just in case. Sometime tomorrow I'd head into the Village, find an internet café and soak it all up.

**

The lights at the NYPD's headquarters at 1 Police Plaza never went out, but in the office of First Deputy Commissioner Frank Garvey only a desk lamp illuminated the room. The first light of dawn was still a few hours away. Buster Campbell blended into the darkness. He was barely visible as he sank back into his chair across the desk from his boss.

'So what is this, sir?' Buster asked quietly. 'A late meeting or an early one?'

He looked at Garvey but his small dark eyes were difficult to read in this light.

'Crime never sleeps Campbell, you should know that.'

Buster nodded. Garvey smelled of Marlborough cigarettes, American Crew styling gel and the cheap cologne that hung about him like his own personal smog.

Odds on he was still seeing the married blonde from patrol services, probably planning on treating her to a hot dog from Rudy's later. He always was a tightwad. Buster and Garvey had both came through the academy together but he had always been a better ass kisser than a thief-taker.

'I understand you've got a contact in this kidnapping caper in the 7th. An English guy?'

'I'm pretty sure he's nothing to do with the actual 134, sir, but he was involved in locating the girl and passing on her whereabouts. As I understand it, she seems to be a wealthy English heiress in fear of her father. She's been hiding out here under the radar.'

His tone was even but respectful. When it came to police work, if Columbo were a chess player Garvey had stuck to playing snakes and ladders since the beginning. Internal politics. Sucking up. Saying the right things to the right people, and taking the 'right' politically correct stances had got Garvey where was today. His specialist subject was insincerity.

Buster wasn't sure what game he was playing now.

'Yes, yes, I know all that,' Garvey sighed impatiently. He tapped a file of paperwork in front of him. 'There are some elements involved in this case that displease me. The mobsters I can handle, but there's a whiff of corruption in the department and I don't like it.'

When Garvey was tired, his Connecticut origins became more apparent as he spoke; not just the glottal stop but also the end t's trailing off. He took off his spectacles for a moment, rubbed the bridge of his nose then reached for his coffee cup.

Buster opened his mouth to speak, but Garvey waved a finger to silence him and carried on, 'Sure, I know it happens, it has done since we were cracking heads in the Five Points, but if I don't smell it, I can live with it.' He leaned back in his chair a little. 'And right now it stinks like dog shit baking on the sidewalk on a sunny day. I can't have it, Buster. I won't have it. And you'd never have it either. I know you've taken some flack from these *elements*.'

Buster shuffled in his chair slightly but said nothing.

Garvey smirked. 'Omerta! From a cop?'

'It's nothing I can't handle.'

'I know that Campbell, I just want you to keep me informed about anything you hear. You're part of this case whether you like it or not, and I think some crooked cops, the mob and even that cut-price Sam Spade from London are all mixed into it as well.'

He must be under pressure from someone on high, thought Buster who stayed silent. Garvey noticed and his tone became more persuasive.

'Buster, I'm not asking you to go Serpico here, just give me something when you have it. I'm asking the captains in every precinct. I know you don't like corruption within the force any more than I do. A lot of us don't.'

Buster nodded his head a little in agreement but added nothing. He didn't think Garvey was corrupt but neither did he think he was much of a cop. Still his life plan had worked. Their careers in the force had taken entirely different trajectories. He was heading out, Frank Garvey was still heading for the top.

His boss waited a beat then sighed again and reached for his cup of Joe.

'That will be all Captain.'

'Thank you, sir.'

Chapter 6

Day Three.
Wednesday 14th May
Hell's Kitchen
10am

I caught the odd glimpse of the Empire State building in the distance, but Hell's Kitchen was some way off the tourist route. I had arranged to meet Andre Schweitzer at his office on West 48th Street which turned out to be at the top of a building called *Terrific Tenements*, named no doubt by someone with a PhD in irony. According to the New York Post, the area was creeping slowly towards gentrification, but someone had clearly forgotten to notify the human flotsam who were loitering everywhere – hookers, junkies and down-and-outs left over from last night's misadventures.

These lost souls decorated the nearby pavements like dumped but uncollected left-over Christmas trees in February. Out of time, out of place and totally out of luck. The collateral damage of the American Dream.

This was Gotham all right.

The gaff looked no brighter on the inside. The lift's 'Out Of Order' sign, scrawled on cardboard in black felt-tip pen, looked like it had been Sellotaped up there since before Rudy Giuliani started using hair dye.

Trust Andre to rent a room on the top floor.

'Welcome to the real New York,' the dozy baldhead laughed as he opened the office door. 'How do you like the neighbourhood?'

'Classy. It's not often I get offered three $10 blow-jobs before noon.'

'It's all part of the service in the city that never sleeps, H.'

The office was dingy and badly ventilated with files and paperwork stacked haphazardly on every available surface. The only decorations were two signed and framed posters from Agnostic Front and the Cro-Mags hanging on the wall, slightly out of kilter.

There was something else that caught my eye immediately. At the back of the room, staring at a computer monitor was a particularly cute Mod bird. Her shiny dark brown hair was chiselled into an immaculate Sixties bob and her generous frontage was packed tightly into a crisp, white Fred Perry. She could have walked straight out of any edition of TV's *Ready Steady Go!* But my immediate interest was strictly a one-way street. She had barely looked up from her PC screen since I got there.

Andre had followed my eyes. 'Hey Shayna,' he said. 'This is Harry, an old buddy of mine from *Lunden tahn*.'

I could tell from his dopey grin that he had a thing for her. The woman gave me the once over. She was a looker all right, dark brown eyes, a nose like Lillian Gish, late twenties, early thirties maybe. A tad too much makeup.

'Hey Harry,' she said curtly before looking back at whatever she was engrossed in. Her tone was odd, so strangulated and Transatlantic she would give Lulu a run for her money.

'Miss Shayna McBain,' said Andre, looking at her with obvious affection from his creaking office chair. 'Born and bred in the heart of NYC with family hailing from Scotland the Brave. So you may have to get yourself Mr Spock's universal translator.'

'That right? Maybe you should call your firm Ba'heid & Bonnie.'

I'd learnt a bit of Sweaty infiltrating a tasty Glasgow Rangers crime family back in my u/c days. Quis Separabit and all that. Ba'heid was Jock for baldhead, but the quip fell flatter than a squashed Lorne sausage.

Andre looked blank while Shayna audibly sighed but said nothing. The room temperature seemed to plummet by ten degrees.

She got up and walked to a filing cabinet. The rest of the view was even better. She had legs that belonged on a catwalk, long and slender; they emerged from her black mini-skirt, tapering tastefully into a pair of oxblood coloured tassel loafers. If my instincts were right, and they usually were, she was wearing stockings and not suspender tights.

'Anyway, this job H...,' he said, jerking my attention away from his assistant's shapely pins. 'We can talk about it on the way. Shall we catch a traditional New York yellow cab?'

'No need for any sherberts, this week mate, Tommy is outside, he can take us. Save your dough.'

'Limo driving all over town with Mr Big Shot, what do you think of that Shay?'

She grunted. He looked at me, raised his eyebrows in defeat and we left.

***

Central Park South was only a mile from Hell's Kitchen but it was another world in terms of real estate prices. We could have walked there in half the time it took by car. What should have been a five-minute drive was stretching out as the traffic piled up. Amidst the car horns and all the other urban racket, I could hear cheery New Yoik cries of 'You believe this shit?' and 'Suck my dick, di Blasio'. There were a few 'Whad ya gonna do?' exclamations from the locals; and 'Fuhgeddaboutit' from a kidult on a skateboard.

'What do you think of Shayna, eh?' asked Andre. 'Some classy dame, eh?'

'I wouldn't mind her blowing a wind around my Trossachs.'

Andre laughed. 'You're welcome to try my friend but you'll be whistling in the dark. I was in a bar with her

49

when some guy tried to hit on her and she just snapped "Get tae fuck!", whatever that means.'

'It's a Scottish pleasantry meaning, thank you for your interest but I'm otherwise engaged... Tights or stockings?'

'Eh?'

'Does she wear tights or stockings? Stockings would be more era appropriate for her chosen youth cult look, not to mention more pleasing on the eye.'

'I've never looked.'

'Ooh Pinocchio, the size of your hooter. Where did you find her?'

'I got a recommendation from someone on the force. I was looking for office help, filing, phone answering, general secretarial, yada, yada, yada, but she is something else my friend. She works for peanuts but she can get shit out of the internet that you would not believe. Addresses, credit ratings, police files... she makes my job so much easier.'

And your wanks, I thought. I'd seen the way he looked at her, all doe eyes and goofy grins.

'Good connections. She ex-plod?'

'Yeah, but she's not forthcoming about it. I ask no questions and she don't tell me no lies. It works, brother.'

'I'll bet it does...'

'Hey, you going caveman on me, H?'

'Like you haven't thought about it!'

'Man! Look, it's just a bonus that she's a bit of a doll. Winner, winner, chicken dinner!'

'Listen to yourself! You lefties always think you occupy the moral high ground, so you just forget inconvenient facts about your heroes. Posh boy Joe Strummer was shafting his mates' wives like sex was going out of fashion and Joe Stalin was jumping into bed with a 13-year-old. Uncle Joe? Paedo Joe more like.'

'He's not one...'

'He's not one of yours, I know. But your boy Leon went over the side with Frida Kahlo and Gerry Healy was Trotskyism's answer to Harvey Weinstein…'

'I know, I know. I'm just trying to be a better man.'

'You and me both, bruv. You and me both. But, Andre, you would, wouldn't you?'

'Shut the fuck up!'

Andre knew he was beaten. In truth, he'd had the hots for Shayna McBain ever since he had interviewed her for the job late one afternoon at the Double Down a month or so ago, but he was never going to admit it.

After a minute of silence, I broke the ice. 'Talk me through the set-up with Johnny Baby again.'

'It's simple. He has got an impenetrable room that he built to store his prized possessions; there is only one way in and only one way out. A couple of weeks back, he had a party for fellow Mafiosi who got to check out the goodies inside. It was guarded round the clock, with an x-ray machine to get past, and yet someone walks in, substitutes Johnny's *precious* for forgeries, and walks out again undetected.'

'Insurance job?'

'Unlikely, unless De Niro has given JB a crash course in acting. He is spitting feathers.'

'And he wouldn't want the cops giving a haul like that the once over, even if it was all legitimately acquired. What's he like, as a bloke?'

'Johnny? A regular jolly hard case, good as gold until you cross him. Giuliani, his number two, is the one to worry about. We're talking psycho killer, qu'est que c'est.'

The brake lights ahead went off. We were moving.

***

'What a fuckin' joint this is, excuse my French,' exclaimed Tommy Byrne as he pulled up outside the six-storey mansion on West 57th Street. He had a point. It was a gaff of a gaff. Crime doesn't pay? Like fuck it doesn't.

'Thanks Tommy,' I said.

'Yeah thanks pal,' grunted Andre.

'It's what I'm paid for, fellas,' the driver shrugged. 'I'll wait outside, up the road a-piece. If you want me, just whistle.'

Andre looked blank.

'You know how to whistle don't you?'

'You just put your lips together and blow,' I said, finishing the quote. 'Thanks Lauren, the years haven't been kind, but you'll always be a looker to me.'

Tommy laughed. Andre still looked blank.

'Lauren Bacall from To Have And Have Not – strewth man, this is your culture not mine.'

'Bogart?'

'Yeah, but never mind all that, look at this gaff mate.'

'It's a beaut.'

We stopped on the pavement for a beat or two, soaking up the architecture.

'I guess Johnny Baby was always going to end up in the Big House... one way or another.'

Andre seemed suddenly spooked. 'No jokes like that inside, okay, Harry,' he said. 'I know you're kidding but these guys don't fool around. I know you know that and I don't need to tell you to mind your manners, but for fuck's sake please do cos otherwise we'll both be sleeping with the fishes. Capisci?'

'Me, you, Luca Brasi, and a few more besides. Yeah of course capisce. This ain't my first rodeo, mate.'

'I know, but...'

He left the words swinging in the air as I pressed the intercom.

'Yeah?' said a gruff voice.

'Schweitzer and Tyler for Mr Infantino,' I said.

'A good name for a firm,' Andre muttered.

'Yeah? We sound like dental floss salesmen from Indiana.'

The heavy wrought-iron gates swung open, and we made our way inside.

Security was tourniquet tight. First there was a hard-faced doorman, fully suited and booted, who patted us down and called ahead for clearance – I noticed that the front door was heavy; it probably had with a solid steel interior to slow down unwanted visitors armed with inconveniences like bartering rams.

Inside we met a tall sad-looking man who would never see seventy again. He asked us to hand over our phones before we proceeded. He then also called ahead, mumbled a few words and waved us on.

We walked down a corridor with walls covered in photos, past what I imagined was the family dining room – there were portraits of people decked out in the glamorous style of the 16th Century de Médicis – and finally we made it to a young elevator operator with a speech impediment who patted us down again and made one final half-stuttered phone check.

All three of the 'domestic staff' looked like they'd be more at home nobbling Nazis in the Dirty Dozen than hounding hot housemaids in Downton Abbey.

The interior décor was out of this world. The place made Highclere Castle look like a dump. It was only the personnel who made you realise this dream setting was more suited to the pen of Mario Puzo than Baron Julian Fellowes of West Stafford.

'Holy shit,' I murmured.

'Ain't that right.'

It took us seven minutes from the street to reach the door of Johnny's penthouse and the last line of defence. The ice cream who opened the door was a heavy-built, sixteen-stone unit whose hawkish features seemed to have been carved from Sicilian granite. He was late forties with a few flecks of grey in his dark slicked back barnet, and his eyes were as cold as a February frost. I clocked the Rolex Oyster and the $30,000 diamond encrusted gold bracelet that glittered on his wrists. This was Johnny Baby's capo Giuliano Clarini. Had to be. The big guy sucked on an obviously expensive cigar, a Cohiba by the aroma. The stogie remained glued to his lips as he looked us up and down. When he finished, he grinned at us in a cold, calculating way, like a crocodile sizing up its next meal. Giuliano's smile never reached his eyes; I got the feeling it never would.

He said nothing, he just grunted, the cheroot still in place, and flicked his sizeable forehead in the direction he wanted us to walk. He was agitated and seemed to have the sniffles. Or at least an unseasonal runny nose. Allergies or substance addiction? It didn't feel like the appropriate time to ask.

I had never seen Giovanni Infantino in person; online he looked harsher than a Siberian winter but here, in the flesh, Johnny Baby was much warmer with an easy smile, plenty of laughter lines and bright twinkling eyes. He too was dressed impeccably but the thing that first caught my eye were his handmade Italian shoes. The way the laces were tied, they looked like little nooses.

'Andre, mio amico,' he said, giving my compadre a bear hug and kissing him on both cheeks.

He turned to me. 'And you must be the famous Scotland Yard detective, I've heard so much about, Tyler of the Yard.'

'Ex,' I said quickly, shaking his hand and noting the strength of his grip. 'I left Her Majesty's Metropolitan Police Service quite a while ago. Strictly gum-shoe these days.'

'A regular Philip Marlowe, eh?'

'I try my best, Mr Infantino.'

'Call me Johnny, we're all friends here,' he said, giving me a hug. 'Ain't that right Giulio?'

The big lug grunted. I could feel his eyes burning into the back of my skull.

I moved things on. 'Andre has filled me in, Mr... Johnny, could you show me the room where the robbery took place?'

'Of course. Follow me.'

We led the way down a hallway lined with pictures that probably cost more than I ever earnt in a year and what my dad had made in a life-time of honest labour. About twenty feet past his office, Johnny Baby stopped at a large bookcase full of what looked like pricey first editions of the classics.

Odd, I wouldn't have put him down as a Jane Austen man. Looks were of course deceiving.

'Andre told me you're a man of discretion,' he said in a tone that managed to be both friendly and threatening at the same time. 'After I show you around in here, you will need to forget some of the things you see. Is that clear?'

'Of course, crystal clear.' I knew all right. Loose lips sink ships and all that, or in this case, shooting my mouth off would guarantee I'd be part of the foundations of the next available construction job.

He turned and removed a book in the centre of the middle shelf. The book was Crime And Punishment by Dostoevsky. Of course it was. And like every other book on display, it was a dummy. The bookshelf swung open to reveal a solid steel door adorned with a gleaming chrome pin release lever, a keypad and a good old-fashioned keyhole for that belt and braces finish.

Johnny tapped in his code number surreptitiously and inserted a large silver key with a theatrical flourish. Then he pulled the heavy door open to reveal the kind of room you would expect to belong to a minted 1960s Bond super-villain with an interest in world domination.

It was large, spacious, and packed with gains that were either ill-gotten or undeserved. The room was oak panelled throughout and lit up by recessed lighting.

I stepped inside and looked up, expecting to see a sky-light in the ceiling, but there wasn't one. There were no windows anywhere. The door was the only way in and the only way out. The room looked like it had been designed in anticipation of incarcerating Harry Houdini once he had managed to stumble out of McSorley's.

I glanced around and yet again felt the urge to whistle. This place would blow Arthur Daley's mind. There were bronze statues and paintings everywhere. To my right, fur-coats in undisturbed dry-cleaning wrapping hung from gold-plated hooks on the wall, and over on the left-hand side were gun racks with enough hardware to start a third world war. A display case packed with expensive Swiss watches stood in the far corner opposite a heavy, medium-sized freestanding safe which I guessed would probably contain more tom, gold bars, hard cash, harder drugs, blackmail photos and incriminating tapes, and God knows what else a senior mob boss liked to collect.

Another display case contained pricey Lladro and Meissen porcelain figures along with what looked like photos signed by Frank Sinatra, Sammy Davis Junior, Dean Martin, Joey Bishop and Peter Lawford. The whole Brat Pack.

Next to them, in an ironic touch, was a 1975 promotional picture of Sgt Pepper Anderson from Police Woman signed by Angie Dickinson – the long legs of the law.

The case closest to the door was open with the Matisse painting and the scribbled page of Bob Dylan lyrics lying carelessly on their side. The snide versions of course. The Sextons. The fakes.

'Talk me through your open day please, Johnny.'

He sighed. 'I had a few friends round, trusted friends, to celebrate my birthday. They knew I'd had this little *scrigno del Tesoro* built, what you'd call a treasure chest, and I let them all have private viewings. We were very careful. We hired a small airport scanner which they had to go through in the corridor outside before they could get in and get out, and they were searched thoroughly both ways too. All supervised by Giulio. It went very well. It was days later that I realised the Dylan lyrics had been substituted and so I ordered a full check and found one of the Matisse works and a $20,000 buck necklace had also been replaced with forgeries.'

His face darkened. 'Look at this shit!'

Johnny grabbed the Dylan lyric sheet and thrust it in front of me. 'What? Does whoever this pezzo do merda is think I'm a fuckin' jerk-off?'

I felt his pain. It wasn't even a good forgery. The paper was brand new and stained with something, maybe tea, and then dried, to give a vague impression of a fifty-year-old document. The faked painting was equally shoddy. Whoever pulled off this job had been counting on Johnny Baby paying little attention to his treasured collectables in the near future.

The underboss got angrier. 'I have been robbed. Me! The indignity! Who would dare?'

I nodded. He was as embarrassed as he was angry.

'Obviously you couldn't go to the cops,' I said.

'Obviously. So I asked our mutual friend here, Schweitzer, to solve the mystery. So far nothing. Let's see if two detectives are better than one.'

I nodded again. 'Understood. Let me establish a few things if I may, Mr Infantino. Firstly, your guests came into this room in ones and twos, is that right?'

'Yes. As I said, they had private viewings.'

'And you don't have CCTV in operation?'

His face turned purple. 'It's being fitted next month,' he fumed, spraying me with spittle.

I wiped it off without making a fuss.

'Do you mind if I talk this through alone with Andre?'

'Not at all. Giuliani and I will be in the corridor outside.'

I nodded, and he left us.

'Any ideas?' asked Andre.

'None yet. The walls are wood-panelled, the ceiling and floor are solid.'

'Yep.'

'There's no window.'

'Well spotted.'

I gave the room another once over but apart from a tiny air vent only a half-starved city rat could crawl through, the door was the sole way in. Hmm. A tough nut to crack. On paper at least.

'The guests were all mafia?'

'Yep.'

'All friends?'

'Yep.'

'High-flyers?'

'New York's finest.'

'They were searched on the way in and on the way out…'

'Yeah, by Giuliani. Some weren't too happy about that but they all went along with it, out of respect.'

'So it has to be an inside job…'

'I thought the same, but Giulio is the gatekeeper and he's solid. I mean, he has done time for Johnny, he's loyal and he's minted. What's his motivation?'

That might be a question worth asking, I thought, but all other things being equal there was only one conclusion to be reached here.

'I've got half an idea of what might have happened, but I need a little time to think it through.'

'Share then…'

'Wait.'

I walked back to the door and waved at Johnny Baby. 'Mr Infantino, who did you use to build this room?'

'Canning Buildings. The firm belongs to friends of ours, the Murphys.'

'Could you call them in again tomorrow please? Mid-morning say? I've got a theory I want to test.'

'Okay. They're out of town, Boston, but for me, they'll be here.'

'Thank you. And if you'll indulge me, don't tell anybody else about it for now, not even people you trust.'

He looked at me sideways like a wolf sensing a prairie squirrel.

'You think you know where my property is?'

'I have a working theory; right now, it's the only thing that makes sense, and I think I know exactly where we'll find it all.'

Johnny Baby's eyes glinted. 'Okay,' he said, turning to Giuliani. 'Make it so.'

The big man wiped his nose and nodded. He seemed happy enough, but as soon as Johnny turned back to face us, he shot me the kind of look that Medusa must have used to turn her enemies into statues.

The bloke was so far beyond pissed it was a wonder his heart didn't detonate. If he had one.

He didn't give off a bad vibe, he emanated malice.

'One last thing Johnny,' I said. 'Can you seal the room now and make sure it stays sealed until tomorrow?'

'Happy to.'

He shook my hand firmly, those predatory eyes never leaving mine. I stayed calm but inside I wondered if I shouldn't have gone with my hunch this quickly.

***

Tommy Byrne pulled up seconds after we left the mansion and I asked him to drive me back to the Plaza via Andre's office so I could drop him off.

'Did you notice how sniffy Guilio was?' I asked.

'Yeah. Are you thinking…'

'I'm thinking Colombia rather than hay fever.'

'A reasonable assumption from what I hear.'

After all that testosterone-fuelled tension, the whisky in the back of the limo looked particularly appealing. I leaned forward.

'Is it okay to have a glass of this good stuff, Tommy?'

'Of course, it's there for you.'

I poured both of us a treble in the posh cut-glass tumbler.

'Cheers.'

'Cheers. What do you Cockneys call this stuff?'

'Gold watch.'

'Of course.'

'That forehead on that Giulio.'

'Man, you could barbecue prime rib on it.'

We laughed, then Andre paused and spoke softly. 'So what's the theory?'

I hesitated. 'Tommy, do you mind if we close the window briefly for a private chat?'

'Not at all.'

He pressed a button and the partition window rose and closed.

'Okay,' I said, keeping my voice low. 'It's pretty simple. We agree that we can discount the idea that JB is pulling an insurance scam, because that would involve the Old Bill, right?'

'Right, so how did they do it and who would you put in the frame?'

'I'll get to the how, but as for the who, for my money the obvious perps have to be someone inside the firm, or someone involved in the construction job, like...'

'The men who built it,'

'Exactly.'

'Canning Construction. The Murphys.'

'Yeah. Tell me about them.'

'What's to tell? Boston based, Irish mob connected to the Malones. The construction firm is a huge money-laundering operation, and they run the usual mix of bars, hookers, and unions as well. Old school stuff. They must have some kind of cooperation deal with Johnny Baby.'

'Where are they out of?'

'Somerville originally but they're legit now; they've got offices in Beacon Hill near Longfellow Bridge.'

'Who's the guy at the top?'

'Little Terry.'

'Who presumably isn't little at all.'

'A big man, much feared, with some equally lethal lieutenants Kevin 'Mad Dog' Madden and Connor 'The Killer' Dowling, all posing as straight businessmen.'

Andre paused, deep in thought. 'Messing with the mob, though… that would be a hell of a risk to take, even for them.'

'Not if you thought that your heist can't be cracked...and your plan was to destabilise your allies.'

'They wouldn't be able to move on New York.'

'I'm not saying they would. But, just floating a theory on the hoof here, what if they had another alliance, either to a rival family or a rival faction within a family, and were working with them in tangent to undermine Giovanni Infantino?'

Andre looked thoughtful. 'It's not outside the realm of possibility. But jeez… that would be such a dangerous gambit.'

'Yeah, but for such high stakes…' I shrugged. 'Just a theory.'

He thought for a moment. 'But a credible one.'

I pressed the button on our side and the partition window opened just as we pulled up outside Terrific Tenements. I asked Tommy to wait while I popped up to Andre's office – Gotham Central – so he could use his savvy to send the video footage to Sir Tim using my email and his phone. Don't ask me how it worked but it did. That was it, the Amelia job was done. Wrapped up. Finito.

Shayna McGob was nowhere to be seen.

'Hey Batman, where's Catwoman?'

'No idea. Off scratching her pole I'd imagine.'

'Lucky Pole.'

***

I arranged to meet Schweitzer later at the Double Down early that evening, which is where I found Pinky & Perky giving him a pasting. We moved on to McSorley's, the plastic Paddy bar. It was busy, riotous and a lot of fun, and any other night I'd have stayed until they put us out with the bins. But this night, I needed a little thinking space, so we decamped to somewhere quieter.

Andre took me to a small, dingy old-fashioned bar called O'Deas – pronounced O.D.s – and if that was a deliberate pun, it was right on the button given the state of the thin smattering of ageing customers.

Most of them resembled Wurzel Gummidge tribute acts club, and there was a pale, comatose scruff-bag at the end of the jump who looked as if he had actually overdosed and gone to a better place.

Or possibly a hotter one, given the look of the joint. Walking in felt like passing through a portal to the past. The place must have looked great once. The bar itself was dark wood with a marble top and a brass foot rail, all of it in need of cleaning. One end of it boasted a 19th century Demilune.

There were vacant barstools all along it but Andre steered us towards an even darker booth, far from prying ears, with cheap faux-leather seating that was the colour of dark chocolate.

The only person even vaguely in hearing range was a long-haired dosser passed out in the adjoining booth.

'Sleeping Beauty,' I muttered.

'He looks like a bum.'

'More like Hagrid's ball-sack.'

I noticed a dark red stain on the corner of the table.

'That looks like rust.'

'Nah, it's just dried blood,' said Andre.

'Yeah? Then God alone knows what the cheap synthetic leather seats are hiding.'

'You wanna eat?'

'What's that? People actually eat here?'

'Drunk people do.'

'Shit. Judging by front of house, I would hate to see the state of the kitchen. It must be like a Petri dish with griddles.'

Andre grinned. 'This quiet enough for you though?'

I nodded. It was time to get serious. 'Why did you say that you being attacked was down to me earlier?'

'Buster got some intel. You've been in New York three days and it seems you've already rattled someone's cage enough for the word to get around.'

I laughed. 'That's me. Rattling wrong'uns like a fifties scenic railway since 1979.'

I paused and thought for a moment.

'So clearly this business is either something to do with Amelia Storey or something to do with Johnny Baby Infantino…'

'Or something to do with someone who's heard a few of your jokes.'

'Good point. I'd say my sense of humour was nearly up there with whoever buys your clothes.'

He mimed being shot through the heart.

'So the question remains, why hit you?'

'To send you a message. Someone wants you, or for argument's sake, let's say us, to back off. Someone with links to dirty cops.'

'So that's more likely to be the mob than anyone connected to our fragrant heiress.'

'That's what I figure. You're being trailed everywhere by two vehicles – the dark blue Chrysler sedan and a decrepit yellow hippy Volks Wagon campervan saloon, which started tailing you just after the first time I took you to the squat. So…'

'They're not connected. Odds on the VW is full of a load of drippy lefty activists, looking out for their gal, and the former must have some mob connection although not a direct one. Maybe someone is subcontracting.'

'Makes sense.'

'I think so. But subcontracting to Jersey and not the Murphys or their pals the Malones in Boston…?'

'Yup. The pieces aren't fitting together yet. What's your theory about the heist?'

'For that you're going to have to wait until tomorrow mate.'

'It had better be right.'

I nodded glumly. It was a gamble, all right.

'Will you back off, Harry?'

'Where's the fun in that?'

I walked up to the bar, ordered two more beers and a bottle of Bushmills, and we drank like Prohibition was due to kick in again tomorrow morning.

***

When the two men stumbled out into the night, Sleeping Beauty in the adjoining booth snapped wide awake and retrieved his listening devices from the adjacent booth and the one next to that. He'd figured the two marks would go to the furthest one but had wired up the other empty booth next to it as insurance. With his gear tucked away in a small incongruous attaché case, he then walked up to the pay phone and made a call.

At the other end of the line, a man wearing a Rolex Oyster and a $30,000 diamond encrusted gold bracelet answered.

'Yeah?'

'They don't know anything for sure, boss. They don't even know who's tailing them. Or why.'

The man sucked on his Cohiba Maduro 5 Magicos. 'Good,' he said, before he hung up. 'Stay on 'em and keep the pressure on.'

The targets were a nuisance now. If they became a threat, they would be neutralised. No problem, no sweat.

God knows why we ended up in a Chinese restaurant. We'd already eaten, and we'd drunk enough for a fleet of sailors. Yet the unrelenting cacophony and energy of New York at night re-ignited our thirst.

To the big bad apple our problems and fears were matters of complete indifference. *Who-da-fuck-cares?* Just get on with it, play the game or move the fuck aside and make way for someone who will.

We ordered Chinese beers and three plates of Dan-Dan Noodles. Andre got to his feet unsteadily and staggered off for a Gypsy's whereupon a Chinese waiter tapped me gently on the shoulder.

'Hey, English, you like a gamble?' he said.

I shrugged. 'Sure.'

'You like greyhound racing?'

'I do,' I said, remembering happy days at Walthamstow Dogs with my grandad, also a Harry but a May not a Dean.

He thrust a folded-up piece of paper into my hands. 'You back this dog tomorrow.'

'Eh?'

'Back this dog! Ten dollar to win at Hinsdale. You can't go wrong.'

I thanked him and he evaporated into the surrounding hubble and bubble. The smells were delicious. I breathed in deep, savouring the mix of garlic, oyster sauce, green onion, soy sauce, and the hint of ginger.

Andre had caught the end of our conversation. 'You ordering more nose-bag?'

'No, it was just a geezer with a racing tip. Hey Andre, how far is Hinsdale race track from here? I fancy a night out at the dogs.'

'Hinsdale? Hinsdale, New Hampshire? Brother, that track shut about six years ago,' he said.

I shrugged vaguely and thought nothing more of it.

Although I do remember looking for the waiter a few times and not being able to see him.

Chapter 7

Day Four.
Thursday 15ᵗʰ May

I woke up with the kind of hangover that just three days ago I'd sworn that I would never have again. It wasn't a hangover that could be kicked into touch by a hotel breakfast; this one called for a full-on junk food cure. Salt. Sugar. Grease. Carbs. More grease. I opened my wallet to check how much spending money I had left after the night before. A folded-up piece of paper fell out, and I remembered the odd conversation with the vanishing Chinese waiter. This was his tip for a racetrack that no longer existed.

I opened it and read the greyhound's name.

Perilous Enterprise.

Jesus. What was this, a coincidence, a wind-up, or another warning to drop this case and go home? Odds on option three.

I decided I'd make my mind up later about whether or not to tell Andre – he was getting a little spooked by the trouble we were attracting and he had to live here. Right now I had bigger needs. I threw on last night's clothes like a skank and headed for the nearest McDonalds where I had one double sausage egg McMuffin meal with black coffee, and then ordered and devoured a second one.

Two more black coffees later and I was feeling as well as a man who was about to gamble his reputation, not to mention his kneecaps, on a wild hunch, should ever be entitled to feel.

Tommy picked me up as cheery as ever. He had Van Morrison's blissful Days Like These playing and I told him to keep the CD going until we picked up my bald-as-Satan associate from the fiery bowels of Hell's Kitchen.

We pulled up at Infantino's palace of ill-gotten gains at 10.30am, got through the vetting procedure slightly quicker than yesterday, and went up in the lift to find Johnny Baby, Giulio and two over-sized strangers in the hallway outside the vault room.

One of the new faces was tanned, powerfully built, and somewhere in his mid-sixties; the younger man wore workman's clothes and was carrying a hefty tool box. I noticed Giulio had a sweat on him. Some might have assumed it was a cocaine sweat.

'Terry, meet Harry Tyler the celebrated London detective and my friend Andre Schweitzer. Harry, this is Terry Murphy and his employee Callum Hannigan.'

Big Terry didn't look too happy, but cordial handshakes were exchanged before Johnny opened up his walk-in treasure chest.

'Okay Harry, now explain to us why you've got us all here,' said Johnny, whose smile had now all but vanished. All of them were stony-faced and I could feel Giuliani's bird-of-prey eyes staring intently at the side of my head.

Time to ride my luck.

'Gentlemen. We all know that a crime was committed in this room, that valuable items were stolen and inferior forgeries left in their place. We also know that everybody who had access to this room that day was not only vetted but thoroughly searched and x-rayed. So it would have been impossible for anyone to walk out that day with Mr Infantino's treasures. Do you agree?'

The room echoed with gruffly mumbled 'Yeahs'.

'Conan Doyle's fictional detective, Sherlock Holmes – the Columbo of his day – rightly observed that once you eliminate the impossible, whatever remains, no matter how improbable, must be possible.'

'What are you getting at?' snapped Johnny Baby.

'Well sir, if I may, if we know and agree that your possessions could not have left this room, ipso facto it follows that they must be still in here.'

'Yeah right. Where?' scoffed Big Terry.

Giuliano, who was watching from the back of the room, now looked as happy as an hourglass tree frog in a fridge freezer.

'Mr Infantino, Johnny, you had this room built, did you not?'

He nodded. 'Of course.'

'A big expensive job, well completed by your associates here the Murphys. Did you have any secret hidey holes installed, maybe behind one of the wooden panels, to house a few other valuables, the ones you didn't want to display?'

'A good idea, but no, I did not.'

'Andre, it's time for you and me to do an Eddie Floyd.'

He looked blanked.

'We need to knock on wood.'

Schweitzer shrugged; he followed me as I tapped on every one of the room's exposed wooden panels. None of the knocks were different. The sound was the same for all of them. Uh oh. I started to panic.

'What the fuck?' exploded Giulio.

'What is this?' said Big Terry.

I felt the colour drain from my face. Andre bit his bottom lip anxiously. But then he pointed out a dark wooden skirting board, made up of brick-shaped panels that only ran along the bottom of the back wall; it was hidden in shadows and mostly obscured by the safe and an imposing display cabinet.

'One moment guys,' I said, praying for a miracle.

I got down on my knees and I began to knock on the panels. The first twelve knocks were the same, but the thirteenth was different. I tapped it again just to be sure and then looked up at the watching faces.

'Brick number 13, unlucky for some,' I said. 'There isn't brickwork behind this, this one is hollow.'

I turned to the two Murphy men. 'Callum, Cal, you've got your toolbox, would you mind carefully removing this panel here?'

Callum looked to Johnny Baby for approval and got a nod. He took a small flat-head screwdriver out of his toolbox and began to gently jimmy the brick-shaped panel out of place. He eased it open in moments.

I dropped down again and put my hands into the hole, hoping against hope that my theory was right. In seconds I had found the real Matisse, rolled-up and intact, the authentic jewellery and the actual Bob Dylan lyrics. I also found two kilo bricks of cocaine. Pure and off-the-block, I assumed. Worth around $50K. Enough to make Guilio sweat for several years.

I glanced up at the watching faces. Only two of them was smiling – Johnny and Andre. The two workmen looked puzzled which left just Giuliani and his perma-snarl.

'There might be more stuff in there,' I said. 'It stretches out a fair way.'

As I got to my feet Johnny Baby hugged me with such passion that he almost pushed the air out of my lungs. Then Andre attempted to follow suit.

'Fuck me Schweitzer, you ain't trying to kiss me are ya?'

'No way, H,' he laughed. 'Not unless you've got gum or some really good mouthwash.'

Johnny Baby liked that one. By the time he'd turned around, the other men were displaying appropriate levels of happiness, natural or otherwise.

Johnny Baby hugged me again. Out came his wallet.

'Andre will invoice my company and split his fee with you, I'm sure,' he said. 'But in the meantime, Harry Tyler, have a drink of me.'

He peeled off five one-hundred-dollar bills.

'Johnny, there's no need…'

'There's every need, don't insult me, take it.'

I complied. He went on, 'Now Terry my friend, I trust you implicitly, I know you were not involved in this betrayal. All I want is for you to get me the names of the carpenters you used on this job, okay?'

The older man nodded. I could see Giulio buffering between happy public face and festering internal rage, and so could Andre. We exchanged a nod and beat a controlled but casually hasty retreat to the safety of Tommy Byrne and the luxury limo.

I shook Andre's hand. 'Another case closed.'

'I had my doubts back there, did you?'

'Not for one minute pal,' I lied.

'All the suspicion falls on the builders, then.'

I thought about that. 'Yeah it does doesn't it but maybe it doesn't follow. The two of them seemed genuinely shocked. So's here's another theory – when Johnny was having the room rebuilt as his personal Fort Knox, what if someone used the cover of the renovation of the room to do the little bit of after-hours carpentry magic?

A case of good old-fashioned misdirection.'

'I hadn't thought of that.'

'I suspect there might be more to this than meets the eye.'

'But for the moment…'

'For the moment Johnny's happy, you'll get paid. So we're celebrating, right? So where?'

'I know just the place…'

Andre's cell-phone rang. 'Hold on, it's The Prince. I'd better take this,' he said.

He went quiet for a moment and then said 'Okay'.

His smile evaporated. 'He needs to see us both urgently but away from Manhattan. I know the venue.'

He leaned forward and muttered an address to Tommy Byrne.

'That was Buster?'

'Yeah.'

'And his full name is Buster Campbell?'

'Yeah.'

I laughed. Great nickname. Cecil Bustamente Campbell was Jamaican reggae legend Prince Buster.

'Al Capone's guns don't argue.'

'You got it.'

***

Just after 2pm, Tommy dropped us off at Sunny's, an old waterfront bar in Red Hook, Brooklyn – some way off the manor. The Prince was already there, sharply dressed in civvies. He was 5' 11" and as solid as Mike Tyson's right fist.

Pushing the boxing analogy, Buster looked like a slightly older and heavier version of Roy Jones Jnr. You could see he laughed a lot from the warmth of his face. But he wasn't smiling now.

He stood up and shook my hand.

'Mr Tyler, I presume.' His voice was deep and rich, the timbre resounding like sax vibrato. It was the sort of voice that could slide the knickers off a nun.

'Harry to you, Buster.'

'I've got bad news, Harry. Your girl, Amelia Storey has been kidnapped.'

'Kidnapped?'

'Yeah. She was snatched from outside the soup kitchen shortly after the pair of you left her. Eyewitnesses have given vague descriptions. Two men, roughly your height and weight, which of course makes you suspects and the NYPD will want to talk to you.'

'Anything else known about the men?'

'One eyewitness said they dragged her into a dark blue Chrysler sedan.'

'New Jersey,' Andre and I muttered simultaneously.

'New Jersey?'

'I've been followed by a dark blue Chrysler sedan pretty much since I arrived. It has stickers in the back window, New Jersey Devils and Twisted Sister: SMF.'

'Sick motherfuckers?' The Prince laughed.

'The same.'

'So where was Tippy?' I asked.

He looked blank.

'The boyfriend,' Andre explained.

Buster produced his notebook and turned a few pages. 'Jason Hatchcock, also known as Jason Hate. He'd left the shelter slightly earlier and no one has seen him since.'

I exchanged a glance with Andre.

'Do you think Hatchcock is in on it?' said Buster.

'No. Absolutely not.'

He nodded, thoughtfully.

'So do you need us to come in and make statements?' asked Andre.

'It's not my precinct and not my job, that's one for the 7th, but don't plan any out-of-town trips for the next couple of days. It isn't public knowledge yet. They'll be waiting for the kidnappers to make contact so they know what they're dealing with.'

'Her old man is loaded. Could be a coincidence?' I offered.

Andre gave a shrug in my direction. 'Or we could have inadvertently led them to her.'

'You haven't got her, then?' Buster let a small smile play around his lips.

'Not yet, buddy,' said Andre.

The smile vanished. 'Harry, Andre, do not get involved. Seriously. I mean it. We've got this… and don't give those investigating officers any shit. The lead detective, Furenzo is, eh…' He paused just a little too long for comfort and Andre jumped in.

'Crooked?'

Buster screwed up his face as if he had just stumbled over a leaking sewer pipe.

'He's, eh, he's a good cop I suppose. Used to work out of our precinct, but if throwing you both in jail would get him a promotion, then you will be clenching your ass cheeks together in the shower block up at Rykers before you can say "don't drop the soap".'

'Okay, understood, thanks Buster.' I stood up and shook his hand.

'Nice to meet you Harry,' he said in a low growl and his grip tightened. 'You stay close now.' The message was clear. He seemed friendly enough, but he had marked our cards good and proper. And if Buster Campbell had small suspicions about us, there was no telling how much grief Furenzo would give us.

'Harry, do you mind if I have a private chat with young Schweitzer here?'

'Not at all. I'll be in the car.'

I looked back after leaving the bar and the two of them were deep in conversation. I trusted Andre, of course, but there was still a lot I didn't know about him. We could have been the pair of Judas pigs who led the kidnappers to Amelia. Which meant either he, me, or someone else we interacted with could be rotten. And I knew it wasn't me.

My old UC spidey senses were tingling.

**

When Andre got back, I played it cool.

'All good?'

'Yeah, just cop stuff.'

'Bear with me.'

I leaned forward, towards Tommy Byrne.

'Sorry Tommy, slight change of plans. Could you take us back to the homeless shelter on the Lower East Side please?'

'Sure thing.'

**

We pulled up fifteen minutes later.

'Thanks Tommy, we'll take it from here. Pack it in for the day.'

'Are you sure? I don't mind waiting.'

'You're a diamond, my friend, but no. Give yerself a night off. You've done enough.'

'Okay but if you want that meal, tonight's the night.'

'Thank you. I'll call you later mate, when we've wrapped this up.'

As soon as he was out of sight, Andre ducked into the soup kitchen and spoke to one of the smiley hippy women who seemed to gravitate here between their psycho-analysis sessions and yoga classes. Two minutes later he came out with an answer. Tippy was living in a squat looking out over Washington Square Park in Greenwich Village. He flagged down a yellow cab and had it circle the block to make made sure we weren't being tailed yet again. No sedan. No Woodstock wagon. No problem.

I was expecting to find a run-down rat-hole, but Tippy's squat was located in a handsome terrace of what must have once been respectable four-storey houses.

'Not exactly Skid Row, mate, is it?'

'What do you think H, you reckon someone's fucking with us?'

I shrugged. 'Probably from day one, but let's have a butcher's.'

We walked down a short flight of stairs to the end terrace basement flat, kicking our way through the scattered debris of old pizza boxes, fag-ends, empty beer cans and dented gas canisters and disturbing my first New York cockroaches.

Someone had scratched 'Free New York' and 'Class War' in the plaster work, just in case the postman had mistaken the address for the back entrance of the CORE: Club.

The door of the flat was wide open, with an eviction notice firmly attached to it. Andre knocked. Nobody came, so he stepped through and I followed. If anything the inside was worse than the outside. It looked like it had just been raided by a mob of particularly pissed-off Green Berets. Furniture was over-turned; windows were smashed and the acrid stench of human piss pervaded everywhere. It was like the antidote to air freshener.

It was fair to say the interior décor was unlikely to match anything you might see in OK! or Town & Country magazine. Garbage littered every room, posters covered most of the windows, smashed or un-smashed, letting in just a minimal ray of daylight, and dust as thick as Daim bars covered every surface.

'If they handed out prizes for best shithole, this place would walk it,' I said.

Andre grinned grimly and stuck his head round the next door.

'In here.'

Tippy Jay was slouched fully clothed on a broken double bed, propped up on the pillows. His eyes were closed and he was nodding his head as if listening to a distant tune only he could hear. The small bedside table to his left was covered in junkie paraphernalia – needles, spoons, cotton balls, a lighter and a couple of shoe laces. All that soul-sapping shit.

It took him a moment to notice he had company.

'Hey, what the fuck man?' he croaked, not moving from his seat.

Andre kicked Tippy's right foot with the toe of his boot.

'Wake up man. Tell us what happened to Amelia.'

'Amelia…' He wailed her name and broke down in tears. 'I couldn't do nothing, man, they just grabbed her before I could…'

'Hadn't you left already?'

'Yeah man. I was outside, smoking a fat one. I saw them turn up and grab her. I tried to stop them. I really tried. They worked me over…it fuckin' hurt, Andre, it still hurts…'

'Then what happened?'

'They turned up here and smashed me and the place to shit.'

His body shook briefly with sobs before he lapsed into a kind of stupor. Either he had just had a hit of smack or he was in need of one. It was hard to tell.

'Wake up ya fuckin' deadbeat,' Andre snapped. He stepped forward and slapped Tippy back into consciousness. The little fella gasped and opened his eyes wide.

'Tells us what happened Jason,' I said evenly. 'Who snatched Amelia, when and where? And how did they get to here?'

'I told you. They grabbed her outside the homeless kitchen, man, right in front of everyone. Two guys in suits. They bundled her right into a blue Chrysler. Two fuckin squares, man, I tried to stop them, I swear, but they worked me over they pushed me through some trash cans and just bundled her right in. And then they followed me here. Look at me, look!'

He lifted his Newtown Neurotics t-shirt to show heavy bruising across his muscle-free abdomen. The needle marks on his arms were self-inflicted.

'There was no talk, they said nothing, they just grabbed her and then they were gone. Gone with my baby, my darlin'…'

His eyes were bloodshot from the beating. Or the drugs. Or maybe just the stench.

'Did they say anything when they came here?'

'Insults. Expletives. Threats. Lotsa threats.'

'Locals?'

'Jersey, man. They hurt me good. Those guys, they mentioned you two. They're coming after you. Both of you. They've got my girl.'

Andre and I exchanged a look. That wasn't really headline news considering what had been going on for the last few days. Tippy started sobbing quietly again but Andre was not in counselling mode.

'You fucked up man,' he sneered. 'Young chick, new in town, all alone – you should have been taking care of her.'

'She's not alone, is she?' Tippy protested. 'She's got me, all our friends, the community, her aunt, uncle and cousin...'

'Hold up,' I interrupted. 'She's got family in New York?' Sir Tim had forgotten to mention that possibly relevant fact. 'Who are they?'

"I don't know, man. Just folks somewhere. Rich folks.' Andre scowled.

'Hook me on a polygraph, man. I'm telling you, that's all I know. We didn't talk much about it. We've got bigger things to worry about. Society, injustice, the world, Syria, Iraq, South Sudan... Big Pharma, Big Oil...everything's fucked, man, the planet is burning, the world is fucked!'

'Yeah, okay, right.'

Andre impatiently kicked over the table next to him, sending Tippy's junkie shit flying.

'You really think you're gonna save the world while you're sitting here shooting cotton?'

Our little white punk on dope didn't answer. He didn't even look up, he was slipping back into a stupor fast. Andre looked down at him in disgust.

'We're wasting our fucking time here, H.'

I had to agree. Andre called 911 and then put in another call to alert Buster Campbell. We stepped out and were greeted by the sight of a freshly cat-killed mouse in a shaft of sunlight on the stairs.

'I'm not religious,' I said, 'but if God did metaphors...'

Andre laughed. He needed to. We waited until the paramedics arrived, and then gave a statement and our contact details to the uniformed cops who got there moments later. The ambulance guys said Tippy was in a coma.

We walked away in a daze of shock.

'What now?' I asked.

'Let's go back to the soup kitchen, see if anyone knows anything.'

'Good idea, I guess.'

We hailed another cab and watched the meter go up in the traffic. There was no tail. No nothing. We barely spoke. My mood and my thoughts were both shaken up by Tippy and his tainted life – the reluctant victim of casual violence and the less reluctant victim of opportunistic pushers. Being a junkie was his choice, I thought. Harsh but true. And what was the point of being alive if the only thing that mattered in your pathetic, self-centred life was your next fix?

More questions came flying at me like baseballs in an amusement arcade batting cage. What did Amelia ever see in Jason Hatchcock? She was full of life. Junkies are maudlin losers.

What would make an English deb want to mix in these hopeless deadbeat circles? Rebellion? Misery tourism?

Why had she been taken and by whom? And how could I make sure that me and Andre Schweitzer were not linked to the rising crime wave around this case? Or blamed for it.

***

We were in and out of the shelter in five minutes flat. It was busier than before and the lentil soup urn was doing a roaring trade, but nobody knew a thing. A couple of the hippy broads had seen Tippy leave, and one had had a short doorway conversation with Amelia on her way out at the end of her shift, just behind him, but neither of them had seen or heard anything untoward. There was no sign of Sammy aka Butch.

We walked out of there deep in thought, drifting slowly towards Hell's Kitchen as if we were on cruise control. Was this my fault, I wondered? Was it linked to me? After all, I'd been followed, I'd been warned off, I'd moved in murky circles. It was a shit-show, a disaster.

How could I break it to Sir Tim? He might be cold and rich but even he had a heart, under all that blubber....

POW!

I didn't hear the shot, but I felt it. The bullet went so close to my nut it would have parted my hair if I hadn't had a number three 'holiday' crop. I heard it smash into the building behind me and ricochet off the Manhattan brickwork. Driven by pure instinct, I threw Andre Schweitzer to the ground and hurled myself on top of him. It took a minute for the situation to feel awkward.

'I wouldn't mind but you haven't even bought me dinner,' he wisecracked.

Not true but now was probably not the right time to argue. I got up slowly, keeping my head below the adjacent Chrysler while I checked around. There was still just one bullet-hole behind us. Working out the bullet's probable trajectory, I surveyed the roof of the building opposite. There was not a soul there.

Andre found the bullet in minutes.

'That's almost certainly a 22 lr,' he said.

A professional marksman's choice, I thought.

'I'll get it checked. You had a lucky escape, H.'

'I don't think so,' I said. 'Five will get you ten this guy's a pro. He was plotted up on the roof opposite, he had pukka gear. If he was using a .223 Remington BD, which would be my guess, or similar, then with a gun that accurate at maybe 80 yards, and there was no wind, so that bullet went right where they wanted it to go. It wasn't meant to kill.'

'It was another warning. A direct one this time. To scare you off. So we get back to the big question, who have you pissed off?'

It was a good question and still one I couldn't answer with any confidence. I reluctantly discounted the hotel concierge. And the two bent cops. And even if Tricia had slipped up and told her other half about our night of unbridled lust, how would he or his gun-for-hire have found me? Or even have known what I looked like? I don't even have my photo on my website.

The Twisted Sister mob were a maybe. But why? Who were they? How did they connect to Amelia? And if it were the actual Mob, who would dare go against someone accidentally working for Giovanni Infantino?

If there was a clear answer, I couldn't see it.

Not yet at any rate.

We ducked into a doorway. There was no sign of any rooftop activity. Nothing untoward on the pavement either. Whoever it was, appeared to have gone.

'We need to get you away from here, buddy,' said Andre.

He flagged down a yellow cab and barked, 'Park Hyatt!' He turned to me. 'Harry, we'll have a conflab later. I'll set up a meet with some friendly faces...'

As things stood that would make a nice change, I thought.

***

Alone in the office, Shayna McBain allowed her ice cold demeanour to defrost. Shit, she felt almost playful. A small smile played across her lips as she bashed away at her computer keyboard while the Mod anthem Millions Like Us by the Purple Hearts played in the background on a small CD player, fuelled by youthful energy – London's spotty teenage East End wail of frustration finding an echo of appreciation three and a half thousand miles away.

But the song and Shayna's good mood were rudely interrupted.

She looked up as soon as she heard the sound of wood cracking and stood up as the office door was kicked in. Two burly thugs smashed into Gotham Central, taking a good deal of underhand pleasure from the woman's startled reaction.

The scruffy smaller guy was as bald as Benny Hill's little stooge Albert Wright; his pale face was criss-crossed with scars, as if he'd been shaved by a drunken blind man with none of Daredevil's enhanced abilities. His accomplice was taller, slobbier and fatter but certainly no prettier or better dressed. His Red Sox t-shirt was stained with some kind of brown sauce and his hairstyle looked like the unfortunate mutant crossbreed of a seventies mullet and a ginger Brillo pad.

They were the sort of pathetic creeps you'd expect to see luring children into the back of an ice-cream van.

'Hello gentlemen, how can I help you today?' asked Shayna, intentionally sounding as bland as Star Trek's Data, as if having thugs smash their way into her office was an everyday occurrence.

'Where's that bald cunt?' snarled Scarface.

'Are you still bedwetting, dear?' said Shayna, affecting an air of concern.

'Where is your boss, lady?' said Red Sox.

Shayna shot him a look of sheer disdain. 'Boss lady? Oh Mr Schweitzer, you mean? I've heard him called many things, but that's a new one. You can find him right now at the corner of 3rd and Go-Fuck-Yourself-Sideways.'

The fat slob growled and swept everything off the top of Andre's desk with his leg-of-mutton arm.

Given the state of Schweitzer's end of the office, it was possible the action made it slightly tidier, she thought.

'Now, now, boys, the action art class is on the floor below. Knock twice and ask for Maurice. He's good with morons.'

The fat slob sneered. His smaller partner snarled.

'Where the fuck is he, hot stuff? We ain't got all day.'

'Okay, play time is over,' Shayna said, dropping the banter. 'You pair of pricks get the fuck out or I'll be wearing your balls for earrings.'

'Awwh! Tough chick eh?' laughed Scarface. 'Well listen honey, we are going to wait here until Schweitzer appears so we might as well all get comfortable. My friend here has got something to keep your pie-hole quiet.'

Red Sox leered and unzipped his flies and played with himself as both intruders started to move towards Shayna menacingly. He appeared to be drooling. She smiled sweetly and reached inside her desk drawer.

***

I needed a drink and didn't fancy leaving the hotel, so I headed straight for the Champagne Bar near the lobby. I didn't need to look at the price list to know that Sir Tim was going to pay heavily for the few liveners it would take to help me through my recent trauma.

Sadly, the old Oak Room and Oak Bar – where Cary Grant had been kidnapped in North By Northwest – had shut a few years earlier. So, there was no elegantly panelled German renaissance style dark wood. The new bar was bright, white, and fit for the Wall Street equivalent of a king, but all the magical sense of romance had gone down the gurgler.

I sat at a table and ordered a large single malt. It arrived on a tray accompanied by upmarket snacks, gourmet popcorn, artisan cheese, dried fruit and the like. The early afternoon clientele was sparse. My fellows consisted mostly of what seemed to be elderly coffin-dodging WASPs. The one exception was a well-dressed brunette who was just arriving back at her table. She looked stylish and Mediterranean; sexy and classy, with olive skin. A bit like Tina Fey crossed with Joan Collins when she starred in The Stud but with a darker complexion.

The black Yves St Laurent pencil skirt she was wearing must have set someone back a bag and a bit; the black Manolo Blahnik high heels were a perfect match and the tight red silk blouse was a bonus.

Judging by the Tom, the woman was more loaded than a fleet of Eddie Stobart lorries. The wedding ring was probably Cartier and worth at least £15K. I'd have put her down as late 40s, maybe early 50s at a push... definitely the youngest here.

Behind me, an old boy dropped his glass, the noise jerking me away from my nosiness. The woman looked over and then looked at me. I realised I'd been staring at her like Billy Bunter drooling over cakes at a tuck shop window.

I had managed to close my mouth a milli-second before she caught my eye. I smiled and she smiled back at me.

Okay let's roll…

I made my way over to her table. He who dares and all that.

'Do you mind if I join you?'

'Sure honey, take a seat,' she replied in a warm, slightly husky tone.

'Harry. Harry Dean,' I said reverting to my real name on the spur of the moment. I offered her my hand, but she ignored it. Instead she stood up and kissed me on both checks like we were Continental. I guessed she probably was, by descent at least.

'Maria,' she replied, offering no surname.

'I see they've opened the graveyard and let the inmates out for the afternoon,' I quipped, gesturing at the rich, elderly Cocoon rejects scattered around the place, a couple of whom were clearly napping.

She laughed deliciously. 'Look at that poor guy,' she said, nodding towards a bewildered looking elder who appeared completely lost. 'He doesn't know whether to sit, shit or call his nurse.'

We both laughed.

'It's certainly not the place to go if you're looking for wild adventure,' she added. 'But I like it when I'm in Manhattan. It's safe, it's refined, and you don't get hit on by deluded dunderheads. Besides, I like letting someone else pour the wine for a change.'

She smiled like a magician with a card up their sleeve.

'You in the hospitality business yourself, are you?'

'Kind of. I've got a little place over in Queens. Bar, restaurant. Nice clientele. Respectful. No idiots. You should drop by if you're in the neighbourhood. It's a bit livelier than here.'

She reached into her designer handbag and passed me a business card emblazoned with the name Silvio's in bold italic, and in a font I believe is called Palatino Linotype because I recognised it from our wedding invitations when I married Kara, aka Ex-Wife number two. The card included an address, a business email, and a phone number.

'Yours or your husband's?'

'My father's originally. My husband has other businesses.' Maria paused and added, 'and other interests.'

If she had dropped that hint any louder it would have woken up the dozers.

She sipped her expresso martini and looked at me lop-sided. 'You're from England, right?'

'What gave it away, the brolly or the bowler hat?'

She smiled. 'I hooked up with an Englishman once. He came from Surrey. He didn't sound like you. You're more…'

'Refined?' I laughed. 'Or downmarket?'

'Maybe in origins but you've got a confidence about you. I can tell you've made something of your life.'

I resisted the temptation to reply 'yeah, a mess'.

'I'd say you were a rough diamond. The people I know in London, and see very occasionally, they're based in Kensington, we eat at Langan's, they took me to the opera…'

'I'm definitely not from the Kensington end of London although I've moved in those circles. Never been to the opera. I have eaten in Langan's and drunk in the Groucho, and all that, but like Shania, that don't impress me much. I'm a Dog & Duck man at heart.'

'You like the good things but respect your roots. I like that.'

'And you?'

'England was okay, but I was glad to get home. Don't get me wrong, I appreciated my friends' hospitality but there's a lot of snobbery, a lot of affectation, if you're moving in those circles.'

'Your roots were humbler too?'

'I'm a New York girl, I like to be among my own people. My own culture. We're more on the level here.'

'Italian?'

'Sicilian. But that was a generation or two back. I was born here. My mom was born here. I'm New York through and through.'

She drained her glass.

'What line of work are you in, Harry?'

'I'm a private investigator.'

'You got your own agency?'

'Yeah,' I said, neglecting to add that it was a one-man show.

'So, what brings you to New York City?'

'A missing girl. But I found her.'

'Yet you're still here.'

'I've been helping out a local detective on a mysterious burglary.'

Her eyes twinkled. 'Are two dicks better than one?'

'When they work in tandem, for sure.'

Her laugh was like sunshine poking through a cloud. 'Interesting. I've only ever used one… detective at a time.'

'What was the case? A domestic?'

'Yes, he tailed my husband and proved that what I suspected was true.'

'You're still with him, though?'

'I am. He doesn't know I know. Neither does he know everything about me. What's good for the goose…'

She reached over and stroked my hand, never breaking eye contact. 'Are you here long, Harry Dean?'

'I go home in three days.'

Her hand retreated. 'Well, that is a pity.'

'Another?'

Her demeanour had hardened. 'Oh no. Thanks but I've got to go; gotta get back to the restaurant. But it was lovely to meet you Mr… Harry, and as I say if you're ever in Queen's try Silvio's for size. I think you'll like it.'

'Maybe I will.'

She shifted position in her chair, her red silk blouse stretching tighter over her formidable décolletage, and looked me straight in the eye.

'No maybes, mister. You make sure you come and visit us. If you ain't been to Queens, Harry, you ain't been to New York.'

I watched her walk out of the bar with a wiggle that would have put Jayne Mansfield to shame and then sat and nursed my whisky. No wonder the call the States the land of opportunity.

Bored and looking through the maps on the way over I had noticed that New York State is home to cities called Sugar Bush, Climax and Cumminsville. I think I'd just met all three of them personified.

I was tempted to order another malt, but thought better of it.

***

I went back up to my room about an hour after Maria left, fortified for a call I wasn't looking forward to making. The voice that answered was brief and business-like.

'Storey.'

'It's Harry Tyler, Sir Timothy. I'm afraid I'm the bearer of bad news.'

'Go on.' Still gruff.

'It's Amelia, sir. It appears that she has been kidnapped.'

There was no response.

'Has anyone tried to contact you. Perhaps with a ransom demand.'

'Not yet.' He sounded more disgruntled than alarmed.

'Well, I'm going to look into it, I will find her.'

'No,' he said crisply. 'Don't. Stand down Mr Tyler. This is a different job and one I suspect requires local knowledge.'

'I'm working with a local guy…'

'No. Listen. You will stand down. I know people in New York, skilled kidnap specialists, who I will contact. Thank you for your hard work in finding her but stay off the case. That's an instruction.'

The phone went dead. New York kidnap specialists? I'd have to check out their page in the Big Apple equivalent of the Yellow Pages. Who the fuck had ready access to kidnap specialists, skilled or unskilled?

Fucking Sir Tim. The English upper classes were something else. That wasn't the old stiff upper lip, though, that was something darker. Guile? Duplicity? Insider knowledge? Guilt? No surely not, but something here stank worse than Tippy's squat. What had seemed a perfectly straightforward job only a day ago was shaping up to be something murkier, multi-layered, and more perplexing.

The phone rang. It was him again.

'One thing Mr Tyler. When you saw my daughter, did she give you anything? Either time?'

'Give me something?'

'Yes, notes, a letter, or perhaps a thumbnail file?'

'Nothing, nothing at all.' I lied. The very fact that he had asked me that confirmed my suspicion that Storey knew more than he was letting on.

He hung up. I called Andre.

'Yeah?'

Wherever he was, Peter Tosh's The Poor Man Feel It was playing in the background.

'It's me. Is Shayna with you?'

'No I can't get hold of her. She must be on DND.'

'Dungeons 'n' Dragons?'

'Do Not Disturb, you moron.'

'I know! Could she find out some details about Johnny Baby's companies, the turn-over, the directors, the works.'

'Of course. Standing on her head. I'm sure that would be easy enough too. It's all in public records. You playing a hunch?'

'Yeah. Gut instinct, with a possible side order of damaging intel. If I'm getting fucked, I like to know who by.'

'Well I am at the moment, so you won't mind if I get off the phone.'

'Lucky bastard. Laters.'

Whatever was going down here, I knew I didn't want to be sitting up here on my Jack playing it over in my head. So instead I picked up the phone and rang Tommy Byrne who answered on the second ring.

'Hey Tommy, it's Harry, is your offer of a family dinner still open?'

***

Chapter 8

The Byrne household was in the blue-collar area of Belmont in the Bronx. It was semi-detached but huge by our standards, with six bedrooms and four baths. It was a warm, welcoming Irish-American household, but with four kids and two young women present it was also roughly as peaceful as the fans in the New York Yankees' bleachers after a home run. My presence seemed to escalate the mayhem until Tommy took control and steered me into the dining room and poured us both a large Bushmills from his home bar. The walls were sparsely decorated with just two items on display in solid, gilded frames. One contained a baseball Jersey signed by someone called Tom Seaver, which I imagined was something of a big deal for a Mets fan. The other was a large photo of his late wife which hung above the fireplace. Her hairstyle suggested it was taken in the late 1980s. She had been a good-looking woman with long black hair, and sparkling eyes.

'My Edie, God bless her soul. Cancer took her, at 39. There is no justice Harry.'

'Sorry to hear that, my friend.'

He touched his glass on mine.

'She looks like she laughed a lot.'

'Life and soul, Harry. Life and soul.'

Tommy looked on the verge of tears but he pulled himself together quickly. He was old school; the 'men don't cry' school.

'Let's eat,' he said, sitting at the head of the table and pointing at the first chair to his left just as the unruly Byrne brood romped in.

We dined on colcannon and beef brisket cooked by his eldest daughter Noreen, who turned out to be the mother of the five young children, two boys and three girls. I would have put her in her late thirties but I could see she would have turned heads in her teens. Even now, drained by the demands of childcare, she still turned mine. She her long black hair, alert hazel eyes, a sharp mind, and an ever-ready smile.

Tommy's youngest daughter, Orla, was a different kettle of trouble. This one, I could tell instantly, was chaos on a stick. She was 18 with fiery blue eyes and a mane of tousled peroxide hair that started out as 'strawberry blonde' as her eyebrows. Her dishevelled rock chick look – tight jeans, bangles, silver jewellery, an Aerosmith t-shirt – might have looked lackadaisical, but under that carefree image was a dynamite figure. Not to mention a sharp mind.

Despite the racket, it was an enjoyable meal and all the stress and tension that I had been feeling up to that point drifted away. Me and Tommy talked a lot about boxing, although we disagreed about the upcoming world super-middleweight bout. I had money on a Carl Froch win, he thought George Groves would nick it on points. He was a big fan of Floyd Mayweather, who'd taken the wind out of Ricky Hatton's sails nearly seven years ago and gone from strength to strength – two months inside for domestic abuse, aside; and also the Mexican Canelo Álvarez, who Mayweather had beaten last year.

The only unexpected and mercifully unnoticed incidents involved Orla's shoeless foot that, in rapid succession, accidentally on purpose had collided with my shoe, my calf and finally as far as it could stretch along my inner thigh. I looked startled, she looked amused.

'So you're a Cock-ney then?' she said laughing lightly and purposefully emphasising the first syllable of Cockney. She did it so clearly that I stole a glance at Tommy to see if he had picked up on it too. Fortunately, he was too busy telling his grandson little Tommy to clear his plate to notice.

'I'm Essex technically, but that's near enough.'

'How long are you here?'

'Just a week. On business.'

'Where you staying?'

'The Park Hyatt. Your dad is driving me around.'

Tommy got up to deal with his grandson and her foot was straight back reaching for the thigh.

Orla toyed with her fork. 'So, do you dig rock'n'roll bands?'

'Some. More punk and Mod to be honest. Before your time. But I do like a few Aerosmith songs.'

'Love In An Elevator?' she asked, smiling coquettishly.

'I was thinking more Crazy and Walk This Way,' I replied, thinking if Tommy picked up on her flirtatious signals it'd be more a case of My Fist, Your Face.

'That kind of loving turns a man into a slave,' she deadpanned.

'That's the one,' I said, shifting in my seat. 'Is your name short for anything?'

She smiled. 'Yeah. Orla as in Orla-my-clothes-fall-off.'

I actually felt myself blush and I don't think that had happened since my teens. Mercifully Tommy returned, an ice-cold bottle of Ballantine in both hands.

'So how you enjoying New York, Harry?' he asked, taking the top off one of the bottles and handing it to me.

'Great Tommy, thank you, things are going fine. I've watched enough episodes of Kojak to feel like I've been here before.'

'Hey, cootchie coo!' Tommy said, laughing. 'Quit ya belly-aching!'

'Who loves ya, Tommy?'

'Luckily this lot do,' he said, adding quietly. 'They give me a reason to keep going. Got to help the young'uns get the right start in life.'

Orla had looked bemused by the Kojak exchange.

'What do you do Harry,' Orla said slyly. 'Are you an ex-cop as well?'

'You can tell, huh? Yeah, I was. Undercover mostly.'

'And so what are you now, a private dick?'

I smiled. Either this was the old embarrass the guest game or I had found Finbarr Saunders's long-lost sister.

She looked so innocent too... Tommy hadn't noticed what his youngest daughter was up to, but he was clearly getting the hump with her.

'Orla! That's enough,' he said, his face darkening into a frown like Mussolini's on an off-day. 'Leave the man alone. Mr Tyler isn't here to yap about his work. This is his night off.'

She nodded and clammed up although her foot kept busy every chance she got. I tried not to react. I also tried not to imagine that it was Noreen sitting opposite me instead of a vexing teenage temptress.

We chatted more about sport and TV – I didn't watch much these days, but we agreed The Sopranos was indisputably the greatest show ever made, and that TV cops peaked with NYPD Blue, even if I felt a certain admiration for Vic Mackey in The Shield.

Noreen made Irish coffees for all the adults, hot, sweet and strong. It had all been very pleasant but eventually I wiped my mouth on a napkin and called time.

'Thank you and your family for your hospitality, Tommy. That meal was blinding, my compliments to the chef,' – I glanced at Noreen who gave a theatrical bow – 'but I'd better head back. You know how it is with jet-lag. I'll call a cab.'

'No way, I'll take you Harry,' replied Tommy. 'Sir Timothy has paid me generously to run you anywhere and everywhere you want all week.'

'I know and I appreciate it, but you've been working all day, you've just had your dinner, you've had a Ballantine and a Bushmills. It's not a problem.'

'I can take him back in Noreen's Pinto,' Orla piped up.

'Good girls don't go driving in the city after dark,' snapped Tommy as if she was a trainee nun straight out of a convent school and not the rampant filth-hound she had revealed herself to be.

That was that, though. Orla clammed up. Tommy's word was final. Then Noreen called me a cab which turned out to be another limo from his company, and ten minutes later she bade me a weary farewell. I shook Tommy's hand and received a hug from Orla that was half body-lock and half criminal molestation.

'See you around Harry,' she whispered in my ear.

I don't think so, I thought.

***

Shayna McBain walked down the street briskly. Her face was hard and her pace determined. Nobody she passed had time to notice the few flecks of blood that were splattered across her sage green MA-1 flight jacket. Or the ones that remained on her left cheek and the knuckles of both hands. Just outside a bodega she made a very short call on a burner phone then threw it into a bin and disappeared up a side street.

***

Back at the Plaza I had a large G&T delivered on room service and took a sip. I was about to turn on the TV for The Late Show with David Letterman when there was a knock at the door. Who the hell?

I looked through the fish eye cautiously. Orla was standing outside twiddling with her hair and chewing gum. I opened the door and looked around. She was on her own, and dressed like a part-time call-girl. All she was wearing was a pair of black high-heeled mules, denim hot pants and a silk bomber jacket emblazoned with the New York Yankees logo, with a matching over-sized handbag.

'For fuck's sake, Orla! How did you get my room number?'

"In New York we got a way of doing things that folks outside of town just don't understand, Harry, my dear.'

She smiled broadly. I didn't.

'I don't suppose your old man would be too happy to know where you are now.'

'He thinks I'm at a house party with a group of friends.'

'And yet here you are.'

'I won't tell him if you don't.'

She had a small tattoo on her wrist that I hadn't noticed before. A dove merged with a fish over a cross with the word 'Faith' underneath it. I wondered how many commandments she had yet to break.

'What would he say if he knew?'

'He wouldn't like it. The Lord might be plenteous in mercy and truth but Papa, good Catholic though he is, would probably want to twist your nuts in a knot if he found out anything had happened between us.'

Orla paused and looked me straight in the eye. Her stare was defiant and deliciously sexy.

'So, Harry, either way you're going to get fucked! Might as well be the nice way.'

Jesus, this kid.

In another life I would have probably shrugged and got on with the job in hand gleefully, but nothing about this felt right.

'No Orla, sorry. You're lovely, but I'm too old and too heavily invested in a relationship back home to do this.'

Her face dropped like JP Morgan stock prices.

'Hot and gorgeous though you are...'

She smiled.

'You think?'

'I know.'

'I like men who are older. They understand me more and they know how to get me off. I would be the soul of discretion...'

Yeah, I thought. About as discrete as the paparazzi.

'It would be a dream,' I said carefully. 'But honestly, no. No thank you. Maybe next time I'm here, a few years down the line…'

Orla shrugged. 'Okay cutie, your loss. But could I use the bathroom before I go?'

'Why not?'

She was in there quite a while. I was ten minutes into The Late Show and onto my second G&T by the time she came out. I stood up and she kissed my cheek.

'Are you sure?' she said, her right hand making straight for my groin.

'I'm sure,' I said, as I grabbed it. 'Double sure.'

She shrugged, kissed my cheek again and whispered in my ear. 'Bye bye then 'Arry darlin', it was nice knowing you.'

Something in her voice felt odd, but I put that down to the gin.

I shut the door and hit the mini-bar. Again.

Chapter 9

Day Five
Friday 16th May

4am. I shot up in bed as if some passing angel had just revived me with a $3,000 defibrillator. A powerful shot of adrenalin was surging full my body. What was going on? I breathed in slowly to a count of four, held it and then breathed out to a count of six three times in a row to calm myself, and then I listened intently. Nothing. No human activity was detectable.

But something wasn't right. My subconscious had been playing around with unexplained mysteries. I carried on breathing deeply and let the pieces of the puzzle come to me through a hung-over haze. The mental itch had started when I'd had a gypsy's. Orla had just left the room and yet the bog had been odourless. There were no smells evident whatsoever, neither shit, piss nor air freshener.

So what the hell had she been doing in there all that time?

Then there was that 'nice knowing you' line. Innocent enough written down, but the way she said it felt skewered. I groaned. Christ, my head felt like I'd been hit by the Brooklyn rush-hour F Train but I had to follow my instincts. I had to walk this through.

I started in the khazi. There was still no smell, and no sign of any activity in the room at all other than my own.

I sat on the porcelain throne to take in my surroundings from a different angle. Almost immediately I noticed that the bin wasn't in the right place. The chambermaid always left it square with the edge of the sink and now it was tucked further underneath it. I got up and bent down to check that I hadn't been sick in it overnight. I hadn't. But something else was different –

something had been taped to the underside of the sink. I dropped down onto my knees to look closer. A small tightly wrapped parcel was attached. Using a hotel flannel as a glove substitute, I pulled it off gingerly and cut it open carefully with my travel scissors.

I knew what the white powder inside looked like. Could it be? I dipped a finger into it and dabbed a little on the inside of my gums. It tasted bitter and the numbness set in almost immediately. Yep. Cocaine, and pretty near pure as well. At least eight grams of uncut Charlie.

That was a class C felony here. Criminal Possession of a Controlled Substance in the Fourth Degree. If you were lucky, you'd get banged up for a year or two, but with the wrong judge you'd be looking at 15 years in Rikers.

Orla! Setting me up! Behind her dad's back! But working for who?

Thinking that through would have to wait. I had to move fast. I removed the bin bag, dropped the parcel into it, slung on a robe and headed for the cleaners' cupboard along the corridor, around the first corner. The cleaners wouldn't start for a couple of hours, and the cupboard door was unlocked – guests staying at gaffs like this did not need to nick bog rolls or the hotel soap.

Still moving quickly, I concealed my surprise present behind a couple of bottles of bleach in the far left-hand corner. I'd retrieve it and get shot of it later. All that mattered now was getting it away from me.

I was back in my room in less than four minutes and sleeping soundly in five.

***

Two hours 35 minutes later

I didn't so much wake up as come to. Christ. My head felt like Tyson Fury had been using it for bag drills. The bastards knocking on my hotel door didn't help. By the time I'd got up out of bed, the door was flying open courtesy of a hotel night manager's pass key. Two fat smug New York detectives burst in with uniformed back-up. Andre's dancing partners from the Double Down.

'Stay there!' barked the first cop who identified himself as Detective Sgt Bob Delaney and pushed me back onto the bed. His boss, Lieutenant Furenzo, smiled.

'What do you want?' I asked, evenly.

'We're acting on information received,' grunted Delaney.

The uniformed officers made a play of searching the whole room but the fat detectives went straight for the bathroom. They emerged five minutes later looking red-faced, sweaty, and considerably less smug.

'Why are you here, and why are you disturbing my sleep?' I said in the calmest and most reasonable tone I could manage.

'Have you searched his suitcase?' snapped Furenzo, ignoring my question.

'Empty,' grunted the first cop.

'His drawers, his pants?'

'Just clothes in the drawers, boss. Passport and wallet in the safe. Nothing else.'

Delaney pulled him close and said 'No USB stick? No blow?' in a stage whisper.

'Negative boss.'

'You're coming down the station, pal,' snapped Delaney. 'Get the cuffs on him, Capuccio.'

One of the uniforms stepped forward. I stood up and said very calmly, 'On what charge, detective Delaney? What crime have I committed? I have access to a hot-shot Manhattan lawyer who I promise you will sue your sorry ass from here to Champlain for false arrest. You haven't got just cause, you haven't informed me why you're here, you have no reasonable grounds to believe I'm involved in a crime. You've used excessive force. I could go on, and you know I could because as I suspect you know I'm a former police officer and I happen to know a bit about the law. And about police negligence and the rights I have, even as a legal alien, under New York law.'

Delaney looked flustered, Furenzo was just angry. He moved his hand inside his suit jacket around about where his shoulder holster would be. Was he thinking of a drastic response? Eliminating the problem and then fitting me up? The odds weren't good. I was unarmed, undressed, and outnumbered four to one.

Make that four to two.

At that precise moment Buster Campbell appeared at my door. Finally some sunshine.

'What have we got here, an NYPD slumber party,' I quipped? The Prince rightly ignored me.

'What is this Furenzo? Why are you, Delaney, Clapp and Capuccio bothering this upstanding citizen?'

'Acting on a tip-off,' grunted Clapp.

'What's it to you, Captain Campbell?' seethed Furenzo. 'This ain't your precinct. This ain't your case.'

'That's where you're wrong Bob. Harry Tyler is my case. Mr Tyler is an English detective who is helping me on a highly sensitive kidnapping investigation. I have been assigned to assist him by First Deputy Commissioner Frank Garvey. So you can go ahead and make a fool's arrest if you want but if you do, you can bet your sweet ass it'll be your head on the block.'

Delaney scowled. Lieutenant Furenzo shot Buster a look that could have withered prunes. The cogs in his brain were almost audibly whirling. Finally he grunted 'With me' and the four cops left the room together. Capuccio kicked the door on the way out. Which was both peevish and pointless as it wasn't my door.

The Prince shook his head. 'Sorry about the surprise party, Harry,' he said.

'Some party, they didn't even bring cake.'

Campbell smiled.

'But they did send some coke ahead. Sling us over that dressing gown please pal, and I'll take you to the 'present' they tried to set me up with.'

Moments later we were in the cleaners' cupboard and, using a handy dusting cloth, I passed him the bin liner containing the parcel of cocaine.

'Sweet Jesus, is that what it looks like?'

'It certainly is boss. As pure as I've seen for a while. They had an accomplice attach it to the underside of my bathroom sink.'

'An accomplice?'

A wry smile played around Buster's lips.

'An uninvited guest, who had made my acquaintance briefly earlier yesterday.'

'An uninvited female guest?'

'Am I that transparent? Yes, a young lady whose father is a new friend and if my instincts are right – and they usually are – he will go ape shit if or when I tell him.'

Of course, I could be wrong, the parcel could have been planted by someone on the hotel cleaning staff, possibly even Valeria, the nice Puerto Rican chambermaid, but the way Orla was and her mysterious long visit made her the odds-on favourite by a country mile.

'How come you got here at this ungodly hour, Buster?'

'We've put a watch on Capuccio and Delaney. Thanks to trusted men in their precinct, I am privy to all of their comings and goings. They've got orders to keep me informed day or night.'

'Thank fuck for that. Can I buy you breakfast?'

'I'll take a raincheck, Harry. It's more important to get this Class A packet tested for prints. With any luck one of the dumb fucks will have left their mitts on it.'

I shook his hand and got back to the room, worrying slightly that the only prints would be Orla's. Would she have a record? It's possible. But why should I fret? She'd tried to get me nicked.

It was now 7.17. My head started to throb again, so I drank coke from the mini-bar and ordered breakfast – lots of it, eggs, bacon, toast and enough coffee for four people. Then I showered and got dressed slowly, fearing any sudden movement might feel like the morning express train reversing over my fragile noggin.

It was only then I saw the message light on the hotel phone was flashing. I pressed play and recognised Shayna McBain's voice. 'The blood is in the water,' she said. 'The sharks are coming. Watch your back.'

Better late than never.

Breakfast came by 7.45. I signed for it and gave the kid two bucks. Then he produced an envelope from his inside pocket and lingered a moment longer, no doubt hoping for another tip. I nodded and shut the door. I wasn't feeling that generous. It wasn't like he brought me something useful like Dilaudid.

Someone had tried to set me up. The circumstantial evidence was enough to put me away but who planted it? Once you eliminated Tricia and Valeria the chamber maid, all the evidence was pointing at Orla, Tommy's daughter. But why? Let's say Plan A had been she would come to my room as a honey trap to be filmed or pictured, somehow, possibly for the purposes of blackmail or more likely just to make me leave the country. Plan B, if that failed, was setting me on a heavy possession charge and prolonging my stay albeit in less pleasant surroundings.

So was Orla working for the same people who were behind the attacks? And if so was Tommy in on it? In my u/c days I would not have trusted anyone. Maybe I was going soft. I was the last person who should be taking people at face value.

I opened the envelope. It contained a message from Andre asking me to meet him at Otto's Shrunken Head on E 14th Street at 4pm. The note, jotted down by a receptionist said: 'Can't do earlier. Odd case. Plenty of bees and honey.'

Well he was trying. I demolished the breakfast, cursing the Yanks for their inability to serve decent bacon rashers. It's always streaky, and it's always ladled with enough grease to stop a sprinter's heart at thirty paces. Then I booked a 2.30pm wake-up call and went back to sleep.

***

London. 5.15am, local time.
The multi-millionaire toyed with the crumbling red house brick on his desk as he spoke to the angry American, pouring on layers of smooth, old-school upper-crust charm like warm cream on a hot apple pie as he tried to placate the caller at the other end of the phone line. So far, unsuccessfully.

Reasoning with the coked-up arsehole had become a challenge, like trying to teach a warthog to waltz. He would have to go. Yet for now Sir Timothy Storey kept trying.

'I appreciate that, of course I do,' he smarmed. 'He came highly recommended. His career in the police was a little chequered but as a private investigator I trust him implicitly. If he has suspicions, it might be due to your people's heavy-handed reactions. But I know my man has bought into my narrative and won't betray our deal. My only hope is that your man Schweitzer is equally compliant.'

The long-distance caller on the line from New York was turning the air blue, but safe in his town house in the heart of Belgravia, Storey remained cooly detached.

'I understand. I'm not entirely happy with the situation myself. There is the small matter of my daughter's whereabouts to contend with. You still have her, correct?'

The phone wires burned with a selection of expletives; Sir Tim held it slightly away from his ear until the torrent of abuse subsided.

'If my tone offended you, then of course I offer my most sincere apologies but this matter must be brought to some kind of conclusion and I would greatly appreciate any assistance that you can provide when I arrive later today. I'm sure it will be of benefit to both of us. Remember, we have much bigger fish to fry.'

The voice on the other end of the phone seemed placated. Sir Tim offered Giulio a few more soothing words and listened to him rant. Storey sighed. This was definitely one situation he couldn't trust his hot-headed Wop partner to manage. He heard the mansion's doorbell chime in the background and flicking on a small monitor on his desktop. There were two figures standing on his doorstep. Unknowns.

'Yes, yes,' he said softly into the phone. 'Listen, this can all be resolved to our mutual satisfaction. I will be coming over to deal with all the loose ends personally, okay. And now if you'll excuse me I really do have to go and attend to another matter.'

Sir Tim hung up and sat for a moment staring at the monitor before he got up from his chair. He put the brick, a souvenir from the house he'd grown up in, back on the mantelpiece. Never forget your roots, he thought. Or your needs. There was one small pleasure to enjoy before he left.

He felt his heartbeat increase and his manhood harden. Anticipation was kicking in. He'd given Sourek, his gentleman's gentleman, the day off for this…

When he opened the front door, a poorly dressed middle-aged woman was standing there with a skinny young girl cowering by her side. Both of their heads were bowed. The woman glanced up. Her face looked drawn. He noticed the streaks of grey that ran from her temples to the back of her slicked-back hair and the redness around her pale blue eyes. She'd been crying, and she looked sick with guilt and probably desperation, but she still she accepted a brown envelope from Sir Tim.

'Go inside with the nice gentleman,' she said as she pushed the girl forward; her accent was Kent borders. Pikey, he thought. The child looked at her mother with a mix of fear and anger but she went inside.

***

Cheery Tommy Byrne got me to Greenwich Village quicker than I expected. I didn't mention anything about his daughter's visit, and nor did he. If he knew, he was giving nothing away. I helped myself to breakfast Scotch and sat back quietly. We reached Otto's Shrunken Head at 3.50pm, ten minutes before the Tiki bar opened so I was hanging about outside, cursing the fine rain. I noticed a flyer for a 'Brain teaser trivia quiz' in a local bar taped to a lamppost. Could they possibly offer a tougher teaser than the situation I found myself in?

'Yo! Early bird!' Andre called as he came strolling into view.

'My man. Well, you know me and rum. I can't keep away.'

'Fuck H, you smell like a night out in Jersey.'

'I had one whiskey in the limo!'

'And a skinful last night.' Andre grinned. He looked at his watch. 'We've got a few minutes yet.'

'I've had a bit of a problem.'

'What?'

'Someone left a parcel of Charlie in my hotel room.'

'It's not there now?'

'Buster has it.'

'How?'

'He paid me a visit, shortly after your fat mates from the Double Down, Delaney and Clapped-out turned up in my hotel room with their boss.'

'Furenzo?'

'Yeah.'

'What the fuck!?'

'I'll explain but there's another thing.'

'Go on.'

'Sir Tim asked me if Amelia had given me thumbnails.'

'Containing what?'

'He never said. I told him no, but I've got the USB stick back at the Plaza. Can Shayna do her magic?'

'You think it's incriminating?'

'I think it must be, or why is he asking?'

'It would explain why they ransacked the squat.'

'Wouldn't it just? And why they rifled my room.'

We exchanged pensive looks.

'So what was your job?' I asked finally.

'Babysitting.'

'Eh?'

'Kind of. This big-shot real estate investor hired me for the day to take his 19-year-old daughter to NYU in the Village, while her mom was away at some beauty conference. Apparently, crime on or around the campus has been surging, and he wanted someone to get her there and back, ride shotgun and generally keep a watchful eye on any punks inside or outside.'

'Look at you, half Batman, half Carol Brady.'

'Edith Bunker, please. But think twice about pushing this analogy H, because this guy paid in cash, and I'm buying... if you play your cards right.'

'Well look who it is. Cagney and Lacey.'

It was Clapp with Delaney and another two over-blown fifty-something guys. Presumably cops too. All four of them had their billy clubs drawn. Not good odds.

I looked at Andre. 'Let's bounce.'

We turned and started to leg it only to see another three burly but slightly younger blokes on the corner of E14 and Avenue B glaring at us. They didn't look like cops but had clearly invited themselves to the party. Seven against two. Shit on a shitty stick.

The traffic had come to a grid-locked standstill, so I dashed over the road heading for the 14st Loop with Andre in close pursuit. The three slim mystery men followed suit, getting ahead of us; the fat cops waddled across to our rear. We were getting bookended again.

***

Bob Delaney pulled out his Glock 19. 'This time they're going down,' he said.

'Not here, not now,' snapped Eugene Clapp.

'But...'

'Witnesses, you dummy. We say they pulled, thirty by-standers take the stand and swear on the holy bible that they didn't...'

Scowling, Delaney holstered his handgun and got out his billy club again instead.

***

The bent Old Bill had nightsticks but the three unknowns were unarmed so I headed towards them. Big mistake. These guys had blades. We made an abrupt u-turn and ran towards the fat cops instead. The first of the two policemen I didn't recognise had a kind of paedo vibe – puffy face, pursed lips, bad combover.

The combination of sweat and rain made his hair look like depressed Candyfloss. He looked about 15stone and most of that was in his gut. He swung his club like I knew he would, left to right. I twisted my upper body backwards so it would fly past me and slammed a hard left into his lower back for an on-target kidney punch, followed by a sidekick that left him sprawling on the sidewalk.

His buddy charged at Andre like an irate bull, but Schweitzer took out him out clean with an uppercut. Two down. Five to go. Delaney and Clapp were a more formidable combo though, and I could hear the other three younger men coming up fast behind us.

There was no way we could win this. No way at all.

Or there wouldn't have been if the ICF firm hadn't turned up. Five of West Ham's finest unretired hooligans, my new pals from the flight over, appeared from nowhere, through the fumes of the stagnant traffic, materialising like the Angels of Mons on a First World War battlefield. *Angels with dirty faces at any rate.*

Now the odds looked better. Clapp and Delaney retreated sharpish and so all seven of us were now facing the three knifemen. Me and Andre didn't get a look in. Mad Billy Ames hurled an unopened can of coke straight into the face of the nearest foe whose nose shattered and erupted like Vesuvius, bathing his oppos in claret. Terry 'Badoe' Cosby, a jiu jitsu black belt from Poplar, put a second mug on his back with a savage roundhouse kick and the third guy shot off like a greyhound on benzoylecgonine.

All five of the lads steamed into the disorientated pair with reckless glee, punching them sparko.

Mad Billy helped himself to their wallets.

'For the whip,' he said, with a wink.

'Keep the money, Bill, but give us the IDs,' I said.

Ames obliged, handing me their driving licences. He pocketed their blades as well.

'We'd better move before more Feds turn up,' cautioned Andre.

True. Someone in the hellish traffic stalemate would have called this in. We crossed back over the street.

'Thanks fellas.'

'No problem, Harry,' said Cosby. 'It's the first action we've had since we got here. Shame they didn't put up more of a fight.'

'What were you doing round here anyway?'

'Agnostic Front are playing a hush-hush gig at Otto's tomorrow night, they're mates of Stevie Whale and the Business, so we've come to get tickets.' said Ames. 'Fancy a beer in there now?'

'We can't, Bill. We need to make ourselves scarce.'

'Yeah, more of them will turn up soon,' said Andre.

''Appy days! 'Ope they come looking in 'ere for yer.'

We shook hands and separated. Me and Andre made our way to the14 St-Union Square subway. Heads down, moving fast, but not so fast as to show out.

'Those other three guys, do you think they could be from the dark blue Chrysler sedan?' asked Andre.

'Possibly. If they're not cops, that would make sense.'

'They're no cops I've ever seen.'

'We'll have a butcher's at their IDs when we're somewhere safe.'

'We need to get out of here fast, my friend.'

'I know just the place.'

He looked puzzled. 'You know a place? In my town?'

I produced Maria's business card. 'This is way off manor, we'll get some peace there.'

He studied it and nodded. 'Good call. Nobody will think of us turning up in fucking Queens.'

'I'll call Tommy Byrne to come and pick us up.'

'Maybe don't.'

'No?'

'We don't know who to trust Harry. Tommy seems okay but let's not take any unnecessary chances. Make your own way there and I'll meet you inside at 17.30 on the dot. I've got to meet up with Shayna, make some calls and think of a reason not to visit my accountant.'

'I'll take the subway.'

'Good idea. It'll take you a while and there are a few changes to make, so you'll be able to check if you've got a tail.'

'Okay.'

'And H, change your clothes too.'

I nodded. He walked off, and I went and bought a cheap grey 'I Love NYC' hoodie. Who was going to look twice at a dumb tourist with a piss-poor fashion sense?

***

20 minutes later.

Giuliano Clarini and Kevin Malone were having an argument in the back storeroom of a Hell's Kitchen bodega. In truth it was less of an argument and more of a one-way tirade. A few of Malone's boys tried to look menacing in the background but they knew that Giuliano, who was waving his arms like a Roman traffic cop, could easily dispose of them all if he was pushed much further. Sweat was streaming down his face.

'I give you one job you fucking dumb Mick and you got four muscle-bound retards in the hospital and nothing to show for it,' he ranted. 'What the fuck?'

Malone's brow, already as heavily corrugated as an outhouse lavatory, clenched even more. His face looked grimmer than a Siberian frost.

'Tyler and that bald fuck got lucky, Mr Clarini. And that dame in Schweitzer's office… she's no secretary, I'll tell you that. Not from what my guys said. Something ain't right about her.'

Before the words had finished tripping from Malone's mouth, he knew he sounded worthless and weak. A bad signal to send to this maniac.

'Are you fucking kidding me? A chick?' spat Giuliano. 'You sent cops, you sent your best men and still Schweitzer and that English prick are sticking their snouts into my business all over town.'

The mobster leaned into Malone's personal space until their noses were almost touching.

'I have paid you, you fucking *testa di cazzo!* Get it done. Either they end up in an emergency ward or the morgue today or you do. You might fit in better there.'

Giuliano turned on his heels sharply and moved towards the door. One of the Malone's men, known as The Ox, was close to the exit. He was a big ugly fucker, not much wider than an American fridge-freezer, who looked as if he was carrying an invisible roll of carpet under each arm and walked with a pained arthritic slowness. But when he saw the murderous glint in the Italian's dark brown eyes, even The Ox swerved out of the way as nimbly as a Covent Garden ballerina.

He might have been dumb, but he wasn't that dumb.

Giulio slammed the door behind him and the sound echoed around the room. There was silence and Malone looked cowed for a moment. Then he punched his own palm and snapped out of it. He gave Pat McEvoy an open-handed face-warmer and told the rest of his men to 'sort shit out'.

One minute later, Malone stood alone in the alley outside trying to calm down by frantically puffing on a Marlboro. He held his phone in his hand for a moment, paused a little longer as if he were waiting for some divine intervention – and then he made a call.

***

I liked Silvio's as soon as I walked in. It was a friendly Sicilian restaurant with a large adjoining oak bar, a separate eating area and a vibe that was simultaneously down-to-earth and classy. Kind of like the Cheers bar but with finer dining and no Cliff Clavin, let alone a Lilith Sternin. All of the customers looked local, in the sense that they looked like they belonged here.

I sat at the bar, two stools down from a guy with a Norm Peterson sized gut who had clearly overindulged in the water of life, and studied the menu. They were doing authentic Italian grub for a quarter of the price of the Armani place.

'What can I get ya?' asked the barman whose name badge said Joseph.

I ordered an imported bottle of Bierra Minera.

The drunk's ears pricked up.

'Hey Joe,' he said to the barman. 'We've got a limey in.'

I smiled. 'You know why you lot call us limeys?'

'I do not.'

'Because the Royal Navy used to give sailors lime juice rations to prevent scurvy on the long voyage across the pond.'

'I did not know that! Joseph, give this man a drink!'

Joe gave me a second bottle of lager and I laid three dollars on the bar to let him know I was a tipper.

The drunk wanted to chat but mercifully Andre Schweitzer turned up. He was carrying a briefcase and had a face like a smacked arse. I gave him one of my beers and he cheered up a bit.

'You're gonna want to see this, H, Shayna has done some great digging for us,' he said, patting the briefcase.

I led him to a quiet corner table, far from eavesdropping ears and prying eyes.

'So what gives?'

'This company paperwork tells the story better than I can. Who do you think is the accountant for all of Giovanni Infantino's mob-run businesses?'

I shook my head. 'No idea.'

He produced a sheet of paper and jabbed at it. 'No lesser scumbag than your current employer Sir Timothy Storey, who is also a co-director of most of the companies.'

I was visibly shocked. 'Let me see that.'

I studied the print-out, it was all there in black and white.

'And there's more. She looked up the limo company that Tommy works for too. No prizes for guessing who runs it.'

'Johnny Baby and Sir Timmy?'

'No, that's half right. Not Johnny. That one belongs to a company based in New Jersey which also has Storey as a co-director.'

'The TMF mob?'

'It seems a logical deduction.'

I hadn't seen this coming. 'So even when we threw the tail, Tim and his murky associates knew exactly where we had gone…'

'Because his man was driving us everywhere.'

'Fuck! So when Tommy took us to the soup kitchen that second time…'

'We gave away Amelia's location. We were the Judas pigs.'

'And the New Jersey sedan?'

'The Prince came back on that one. That's registered to a company also run by the Jersey mob. The same company that employs Tommy Byrne.'

'So we've had the New Jersey mafiosi on our tail, and Sir Tim's man driving me on their behalf… so who are the twats in yellow Volks Wagon campervan?'

'I'm guessing that had something to with the soup kitchen hippy mob, looking out for Amelia. Unless…'

'Unless it's someone else trying to make us draw that conclusion, which we did.'

'Woah. This is starting to sound like you're circling around the top of a rabbit hole.'

'Maybe, yeah. But consider the evidence. We've been shot at. You've been roughed up by bent cops who we now know were working with or for an out-of-town mob. The cops and the mob tried to either take us both down a few hours ago or scare us out of Dodge. Someone wants us gone bad.'

Andre sucked on his beer bottle.

'Or they do now that we've led them to Amelia. You've done your job, and they don't want two nosy bored private dicks looking into their business.'

'Here's what I think. That first night in the Double Down you said the mess was all my fault, but you're wrong. I did my bit, with your help I found the girl, and that would have been it, except you dragged me into Infantino's problem and in the process signed our death warrants.'

The colour drained from his face. 'I'd make you right.'

He thought for a moment. 'So Storey didn't want you to find his daughter because he cares for her, or because he's a messed-up suburban control freak, but because he wanted to abduct her.'

'To stop her from doing something.'

'Blackmail maybe.'

'Or perhaps she knows a lot more about her father's dodgy dealings than we know already and it's on the USB.'

'I'll call Shayna now and get her to pick it up from the Plaza.'

'Yeah. I left both your names on it. But I can't help thinking we're missing one piece of the puzzle here. The whole business with Johnny Baby and the attempted robbery could be separate or...'

'Or it could be part of a bigger picture.'

'Much bigger.'

I sipped my Minera. 'This is a lot to process. Johnny Baby and Sir Timmy, though.'

I looked him straight in the eye. 'So how come you got me involved with your Infantino job? I hate to ask you this Andre, but did you know? Were you in on this?'

'Woah, easy H. That was just a good cash deal for me and you. No fucking conspiracy. I asked for your help because I was stymied. Jesus H. Christ, what do you think I am?'

I waved a hand to quiet him down.

'I shouldn't have asked, I was thinking out loud. But it is more than odd that we were working for Johnny Baby at the exact time that Sir Tim's daughter was getting bundled into a van wearing a blindfold.'

Andre went quiet and finally replied in little more than a whisper.

'The robbery was just something that happened. I've been doing a little work for Johnny on the quiet for a while. He thinks there's a rat in his organisation, not really an informer but someone looking to take over.'

'Wasn't that my theory?'

'Yeah, but careless talk costs lives.'

'You've found someone!'

'Fucking Stevie Wonder could have found him. You've only been here and few days and I know you could take a good guess.'

'Giuliano,' I murmured.

'You know it.' Andre took another long drink from his bottle. 'Problem is, how do you tell Johnny Baby Infantino that his right-hand man, who by the way is also his brother-in-law – family for fuck's sake! – is out to stab him in the back to claim his seat at the top table?'

'A bloke he also trusts with his life and a bloke he chose for that position.'

'And personally promoted. But these are dangerous waters. These guys are fucking sociopaths. If Johnny feels in any way that I might think he's a putz for putting himself in this position then I'm dead. If Clarini finds out that I'm going to put him in the frame with Johnny, I'm dead. And since you came to town… ah, jeez!!'

'Won't Clarini have to tread carefully if he makes a play?'

'He'll have to tread like an acrobat in a bank armed with vault lasers. The big players don't like troublemakers.'

'Then the non-robbery makes sense. It was all about humiliating Johnny, making him look weak.'

'And Guilio hasn't got the brains or the patience to have figured that out on his own…'

I shook my head slightly and remembered my old Mum's advice, 'If you can't say anything useful, say fuck all.'

I also had concerns of my own. If Tommy was on the payroll, he would have been like a human tracking device illustrating our every move. Could he have been parked up at the hotel and spotted his daughter making her late-night visit to my room? Had he driven her there? Was he pimping her out as a honey-trap?

Suddenly everything seemed cloudier. In the last few days I'd had bent Old Bill, snipers, some barely legal would-be Mata Hari tart, and a bunch of knife-wielding mystery thugs who wanted to do me in. My future felt as healthy as a Beirut casualty ward.

What was the next stage in my New York adventure set to be? Was Tommy Byrne planning to take me on a nice long trip out of state to the Pine Barrens where the real-life equivalent of Paulie and Christopher from the Sopranos would hand me a shovel and invite me to dig my own grave?

'I know what you're thinking,' said Andre.

'What?'

'That you should of – how d'you say it? – slipped Olga the goldfish when you had the chance.'

I smiled. 'You're so off-target you could be a striker for Norwich City. I told you mate, I'm a changed man.'

'You good?'

'Far from it.' I paused for a moment. 'Andre, this is beyond insane.'

'You've got a point. Even for here.'

'Well here's another point. My glass is empty.'

'To be continued!'

***

Buster Campbell had been wrestling with the uneasy feeling that his luck was running out. He knew there was something rotten in the state of his own precinct, as well as the seventh. Hell, there were rotten apples in every precinct across the five boroughs. And even a slimy toad like Deputy Commissioner Garvey could see it. Corruption had more heads than the Hydra. You cut off one and two more grew back. Which meant the only solution was to kill the beast outright. Lady Luck had come through for him, though. A local drug dealer Calvin McClenic had been arrested a little over an hour ago. McClenic had been a promising rapper known as Big Mac until he found he made more money selling smack than rhyming crap.

The pusher from Southside Jamaica, Queens, might have excelled in his chosen career had he not become a little too fond of his own product. A product that notoriously blunts the brains, drains the energy and rots the soul.

Every time Campbell had heard McClenic's name recently, he half-expected to hear that he had been discovered in some back alley, stone cold dead, and with a needle in his arm.

The best thing about Mac was he also had an uncanny knack of knowing exactly what was happening on the streets. And in the past he had never been averse to supplying Buster with inside info in return for New York's finest turning a blind eye to his criminal enterprises.

Now the dumb fuck was sitting in an interview room sweating about his immediate future facing cast-iron charges of possession with intent to sell. With Mac's record he was pretty much guaranteed another nice long holiday in the jug. If he was jonesing then Buster thought there was probably a slim chance that the offer of freedom might be enough to persuade him to give up some information about any cops on the 9th who were on the take.

When Buster entered the room McClenic was slouched like a life-long 9-to-5 commuter with suicide on his mind. He was so far back on the chair that he was practically lying down. McClenic was dressed head to toe in crisp new sportswear – all black. A white NYC baseball cap provided the only contrast and Buster slapped the cap off the two-bit would-be hood's head almost as soon as he entered the room.

'Fuck da police!' spat McClenic but left his hat where it was on the floor.

Buster sat down. 'Sit up straight,' he barked.

McClenic noticed the fire in Buster's eyes. He hadn't seen that before and it disturbed him. He sat up slightly, just enough to show deference but still maintain an air of defiance.

'Nice of you to join us at East 5th Street. I haven't seen you around here for a while,' Buster said calmly.

'I been too busy licking your wife's pussy man,' sneered McClenic.

There was a day when Buster would have smacked the gold teeth out of the perp's mouth for an insult like that but as Dylan predicted *the times they had a-changed*, and he had changed as well. Beating up suspects carried far more paperwork these days and the IAB and equity and inclusion types were always sniffing around perpetually. Besides which, it was so lame. Yo' wife, yo' mother, yo' daughter… yadda, yadda, yadda. He'd heard it all before.

'The only thing you'll be licking is the end of some old con's winkled pecker up at Attica,' said Buster allowing himself a small smile. 'Face it, Mac, you're small fry and you're going down. Unless…'

'Unless?' There was a small chink of fear under the boorish machismo.

'Well, what say we have a little trade Calvin? You and me. Just between us and nobody else will ever know. Maybe you can give me a little something then I can lose your paperwork and throw you back into the pond.'

'Fuck you man, I ain't no snitch.'

'Bullshit. There are at least half a dozen occasions when you've "assisted in enquiries". It's all on you file.'

'Lies, man. That's all lies. I've never gave you pigs a goddam thing. This is some racial profiling shit right there.'

'Don't fucking give me that,' yelled Buster, who then silently dissed himself for letting his anger and impatience show. 'You've squealed before. You know it and I know it. Another bit of intel won't make a blind bit of difference to your rep but it will set you free.'

Calvin sucked his teeth and looked away. 'Go suck a dead man's dick.'

Buster regressed almost immediately. Right back to the 1970s when the NYC had a free hand to really use 'any means necessary'. He dragged McClenic's free hand onto the table and pulled back his middle finger as far as it would go. The dealer started to squeal loudly. Buster stuck a beefy hand over his mouth.

'Listen you piece of shit, it's late, I'm tired and I'm hungry, so you give me something right now or I'll sling you back in the holding pen and you can take your slim-assed chance of avoiding another six years in the big house. Those old boys will be on your ass like a hawk on a field mouse. Have I got your attention? SPEAK!'

The last word echoed around the room as McClenic tried to compose himself. He shrugged his shoulders defiantly and fought to hold back the pain in his hand but, front aside, he knew he was ready to talk.

No way was he going back to jail tonight. Fuck Attica and fuck everybody else.

'What the fuck you want man? A dealer? A pimp? Whatever. I don't give a fuck.'

'In here. The 9th. What have you heard?'

Calvin spat out a dry laugh. 'You got no motherfuckin' idea man! The circle game! 911 is a joke!'

'What the fuck are you talking about?'

Before the words had even left his lips Buster felt a sting of shame. He really didn't know what was going on and it made him feel old and out of touch. There was a time when he was a young cop and knew every inch of his patch. There wasn't a crime in town that he either knew who was responsible for or knew who to ask to find out. There wasn't a street gang with a crap graffiti sign he wasn't aware of. If a John got his cock sucked on

St Marks Place, he knew whose lips were around it. But as he had moved up the ranks and got closer to 'the suits' he had gradually lost touch with the streets.

He had sensed it over the years and now it had been brutally confirmed. The circle game? What the holy fuck was that? Big Brother was wrong. Ignorance was weakness.

'What's the circle game?' he asked with almost a sigh of resignation.

McClenic knew the old Fed was tired, but he felt no shred of empathy. The way he ran it, he had a chance to taste freedom right now and that was all that mattered. Could he trust Campbell? Probably. Word was he was straight. But if word got out, what was the difference? He'd rather move to Seattle and stay with his brother Gregory rather than take a chance behind bars.

He had been born with a target on his back. None of this was new.

'The circle game man. Some of the shit we get caught with makes it back onto the street. I've seen it myself. A dealer gets rolled, the stash confiscated and then we're buying that shit right back from the pigs that took it off us in the first place.'

'And?' murmured Buster.

'And?' exclaimed McClenic. "And that's all I got. No names. You're the fucking detective. Detect!'

Buster sat back in his chair and exhaled loudly.

'You know that's not enough to let you walk out of here Calvin. You got to give me something. I need names.'

'I gave you all I got mutha-fucker, what more do you want?'

He was rattled and Buster knew it.

'I've got to know who's involved in this. I know you know. So start spilling. Unless you're in the market for a nightstick enema. Your choice.'

'I can't give you what I don't have man but...' McClenic said. But then he hesitated. A bead of sweat trickled slowly down his cheek. Almost. Almost..

Finally he spoke. 'Okay, well man, maybe I have got something more.'

'Well let's hear it,' said Buster quietly. 'I can make tonight's charges melt if you give me something real right now Calvin. I can see the paperwork and those charges dissolving like Doctor Strange had waved a goddamn wand over it.'

McClenic wriggled uncomfortably in his chair and lowered his voice. 'This has got to be on the down low man. I could get fucking iced for this shit.'

He paused again, sighed, and then continued. 'I've heard that some of your guys here are on the payroll of Johnny Infantino but the Five-O over on the 7th are working for some other mob boss. Somethings going down, I don't know what, but you got some shit brewing between both sets of crooked cops.'

McClenic noticed Campbell was struggling to hide his surprise and couldn't resist taking a cheap shot. 'New York's finest?' he sneered. 'Kiss my black ass! You don't know who's shittin' on your own doorstep.'

Buster leaned back into his chair but said nothing. Was he losing his instinct? That very thing that got him where he was in the first place? Was something happening right under his nose and he was buried so far beneath a mountain of bullshit paperwork and reports and petty feuds to notice? A mob turf war brewing on his own doorstep, with cops on both sides, that he knew nothing about? *Jesus H. Christ.*

'It goes up high though man. Almost to the top. There's a journalist chick I know. She's been working with a detective. She has all the dirt. I'll give you her details if you keep your word and I walk.'

Buster swallowed hard. Sure he would let McClenic go. He had given his word. Maybe that was all he had left. But he felt deflated. Deflated and angry.

***

While Andre was at the bar ordering two more ice-cold imported beers and trying not to awake the noisy drunk from his fitful slumbers, I studied the paperwork. It made disturbing reading.

The door to the street clunked open, and I glanced over. Two men walked in. They looked sturdy but overweight and their faces were more lived in than a hippy squat. They stood next to Andre and ordered two pints of Killian's Irish Red on draft. As he walked back to me, they did a very amateur thing – the awkward 'casual' look around. I glanced back at the paperwork but was fully aware that their eyes lingered on me for just a moment too long before they walked off to another booth.

I don't think it was paranoia on my part.

'Harry?'

It was the owner, Maria, looking just as stunning as when I'd met in the hotel bar. Only now she was less Joan Collins and more like a 40-something Sophia Lauren. Suddenly Bob Dylan was playing on my mental Pioneer PL-12: *'Beauty walks a razor's edge, some day I'll make it mine…'*

There was a woman with her with similar features, presumably her sister. She was carrying a bit more lumber but could probably pass for her in a dim light. Twins? Both very pretty, very classy. Hugely sexy.

'Who's your friend, Mr Dean? I do like a bald man.'

'This might be my new favourite bar,' muttered Andre.

'This is Andre Schweitzer, he's semi-house trained. This must be your slightly older sister.'

Both women smiled.

'Slightly older indeed,' laughed the sister, her eyes out-twinkling her gold crinkle earrings.

'By 11minute and 13 seconds. This is Isabella, my twin. We'll come and chat to you and your handsome friend. Just give us a minute.'

I watched them walk away, classy, and elegant. I smiled but Andre looked puzzled.

'Your acquaintance, Maria, I've seen her face before.'

'A wet dream?'

'She's out of my league – and yours.'

I lowered my voice. 'Clock the two fridge freezers at 9 o'clock from the bar, reading the sports pages. Know them at all?'

He took a sip of lager and looked over casually.

'That's odd.'

'What?'

'I don't know them but I've seen them both today. Separately. One was outside my office on the phone. The other got off the subway train the same stop as me. I only clocked him because he'd been reading an out-of-date TV Guide.'

'Clumsy.'

'And here's another thing. Your Maria. I've seen her face before, and it was recently. Where though?'

I downed the last dregs of my beer. 'Well while you're figuring that out, I'll get the bar snacks you forget and a couple more cold ones. Biellebi Taralli?'

He nodded. Nothing much was happening at the bar – the fat drunk was now snoring with his podgy face kissing the stuzzichini – but the dining area was filling up. I put a ten-dollar bill on the bar and said, 'Biellebi Taralli, please Joe, and a couple more Birra Messinas. Keep 'em coming.'

'Altri due,' he replied.

'I bet she does. And what about those Mets?'

He laughed, but when I got back to the table Andre wasn't looking happy.

'Those women, the Real Housewives of Queens, their names are Maria and Isabella, right?'

'That's what she said.

'Johnny Baby's wife is a Maria, and her sister Isabella is married to Giuliano Clarini.'

'Well, it could be a coincidence, the Italian-American equivalent of our Sharon and Tracey or your…'

'Jenny and Jessica.'

'Plus the surname on her business card is Scarpetta. Could be her maiden name, I guess.'

'Who knows? I get your point it could be a coincidence except for one thing. I remembered where I saw Maria's face before – in the dining room at Johnny's as we passed it. It was one of the bigger portraits and I looked at it twice because the lady of the house was wearing black pantaloons, just like Catherine de Médicis used to. It was Maria's face though. 100 per cent.'

I sipped my beer. 'So this is a trap, you think? A honey trap?'

'Maybe. Maybe not. The broads seem genuinely friendly and I've not picked up on any furtive undercurrents other than the two dodge-pots you pointed out.'

I glanced discreetly. 'And they don't look Italian.'

'No. They're drinking Killian's Red. So Irish probably.'

We exchanged glances.

'Boston you think?'

'Who knows? I'll keep watching. Looks like they're waiting for someone. They keep checking their phones.'

'You reckon we're getting fitted up here?'

'We could be, but even if we're not, fucking some made guy's wife is not good for your health in this city, brother.'

He was right. I thought hard.

'She did say she was married when we met before, but she didn't say her old man's name. All she said was that they had different businesses and that he had 'other interests' which I took to mean they had an open marriage.'

'Or so you *wuz 'opin'*…'

'Mate, ease up on the Cockney rabbit, you make Dick Van Dyke sound like Mike Reid.'

'I have no idea what any of that means.'

'I wasn't 'opin' for anything of the kind. I told you, I'm loved up.'

'Harry!'

Maria and Isabella emerged from the staff door next to the bar, presumably leading to the kitchen, with two steaming bowls of spaghetti carbonara.

'Today you drink Italian and you eat Italian. On the house!'

'Thank you,' Andre and I said as one.

'It's my pleasure. You're my guests tonight. You will enjoy many Italian pleasures.'

That smile hinted at more than a Tiramisu.

'Joseph! A bottle of Cuordilava and four glasses please!'

'Dumb and Dumber have gone,' Andre said quietly.

Sure enough the sports-loving possibly Irish lurkers had vanished. So maybe their presence had been pure chance.

Joe arrived with the wine and poured me a taste.

'Just pour, pal. It'll be fine. Ladies first.'

'So polite, these Englishmen,' said Isabella.

'Weren't they always,' Maria replied. 'You like wine, Harry?'

'Almost as much as Dionysus did, but I'll stick with beer for now, thanks.'

A small Italian guy materialised from nowhere with a huge pepper grinder and applied it until I held my hand up to stop.

'Blimey. Does that come with batteries?'

Maria smiled. 'Maybe he's compensating for something,' she said. 'Maybe you don't need to.'

And there was me thinking flirting was supposed to be subtle.

Andre tucked in while the sisters rabbited away about Harrods. Unknown to him, Maria's hand was on my knee under the table.

'Did you say your husband had other business interests, Maria?' I made the question sound casual.

'Oh yes. He's not interested in restaurants, honey.'

'What's he in to?'

The sisters exchanged a knowing glance.

'Gambling,' said Isabella.

'Construction,' Maria said, correcting her, and letting her hand casually caress my inner thigh. She winked at me. 'Gambling, construction, demolition. And entertainment. Now, boys, more wine or more beer?'

'We would love a couple of your Birra Messinas, please.'

Maria walked over to Joe, and bent forward. Whether this was deliberate or pure chance was of no consequence. Either way, her shapely posterior strained against her stylish black leather skirt. It was a glorious sight. Even the old barfly, Norm 2, aroused from his slumbers, was looking on longingly, probably wondering if a swift Viagra chaser could resurrect his chances.

Andre clearly wanted to say something to me, but Isabella started asking him about his private eye work and then Maria returned with the beer.

'We have to leave you for a short while, Harry,' she pouted, pulling a cartoon sad face. 'We're not busy tonight but we have one table in who are family friends so we had better spend a little time with them.'

'No problem,' I said. 'Take your time. We've got all night.'

She smiled. 'That's good to know.'

As they walked off, Andre hissed, 'What the fuck are you doing H?'

'What? A little bit of banter, mate, nothing else.'

'A little flirtation, you mean.'

'She's Italian! Flirtation is their second language!'

He looked grumpy. I changed the subject. 'My feeling is this thing here tonight is coincidence.'

'A pretty big coincidence.'

'Granted. But if it was a set-up, we'd have seen something by now, something a bit more worrying than two non-Italians reading the sports pages.'

'I guess.'

'Sometimes a creepy guy is just a creepy guy.'

'Okay but promise me we'll have one more drink with them and then hit the road. Just in case.'

'Sure. My heart and all my other organs belong to Amanda. I am officially off other women for life.'

'Yeah yeah, well if you excuse me, I've gotta go drain an organ of my own. Where's the *khazi*?'

'Nicely remembered. Ten feet down from the kitchen door, turn left and it's on the right. I cased the joint before you got here.'

'Surely you must need a slash, the beer you've drunk.'

'I do, but I'll wait till you get back. We're not that close. You go and point Percy at the porcelain, I'll get Joseph to pour us a couple of Limoncellos.'

I looked over and Joe was putting his jacket on. He had clearly just finished his shift. An attractive young woman was taking his place behind the jump.

A familiar looking attractive young woman.

Very familiar indeed.

I stood up in shock. Could it be? Surely not. I walked to the bar.

'Amelia?'

She looked up. 'I'm Chiara.'

'You look like someone I know.'

'Oh, you must mean my cousin. People say we look alike. She's English, are you?'

'Yeah.'

'I thought so.'

I looked closely. The new girl looked very similar to Amelia Storey, but they weren't identical. Chiara's eyes were bluer, her breasts slightly larger, her hair was cut differently, her smile was wider. Oddly the cousin looked more like the picture I had of Amelia than Amelia did.

I ordered the liqueurs and headed for the bog.

'My prince has come!' Andre laughed.

'I had to come in here, I've got something to tell you, to prepare you for what you're about to see when you go back in there. Joe has clocked off and there's a new bird behind the bar who looks the dead-spit of Amelia. But it isn't her, it's her cousin.'

'You're kidding.'

'Nope.'

'Wait, I have to proceed this.'

'Proceed it out there. I need a Gypsy's.'

***

When I got back out Andre was chatting to Isabella.

'That's Isabella's daughter behind the bar,' Andre explained.

'She's beautiful.'

'Bella, bella,' said Isabella. 'She's Maria's niece.'

I looked blank. 'So her cousin Amelia is…'

'She's Maria's daughter.'

A flash of incomprehension hit my face. I suppressed it quickly. 'But she's English.'

'It's a long story. I'll…'

'Isabella!' Maria summoned her sister to the bar and chatted to her, occasionally looking over at us.

'Well that was odd.'

'What?' I said, still trying to process the frankly absurd idea that Amelia Storey could be Maria's daughter.

'None of them seem at all concerned about Amelia. They're not worried that she's missing, they're not worried she's been kidnapped.'

'Perhaps they don't know.'

'They don't know? You mean it hasn't made a woman being snatched off the streets in broad daylight hasn't made the news?'

'Exactly which means someone doesn't want it to make the news…'

'We need to ask Buster about this.'

'We need to ask him about a lot of things.'

Isabella walked back smiling with a tray of tomato bruschetta and focaccia, and Maria called me from the bar. She looked exasperated.

'Harry, I need help to change a barrel and move some furniture in the wine cellar before morning, and Joseph has gone. Would you give me a hand please? It won't take long.'

'Sure.'

She opened the counter flap and gestured to me to follow her. I chose to ignore Andre's look of alarm and the knowing smile that played around Isabella's face. I could talk to her in the cellar, I reasoned, ask some pressing questions. Play it cool. Like Del-Boy in the Yuppie bar…

***

We walked down to the cellar. It was immaculately tidy, with not a bottle, box or barrel out of place. The only things that looked as if it didn't belong there was a long white settee lurking in the centre of the room. This must be what she wants help moving, I deduced.

There was classical music playing softly in the background, Clair de Lune by Debussy,

Maria stopped next to the sofa and sat down. 'Here we are,' she said cheerfully.

I must have looked confused.

'I want you to sit with me on my couch, Harry,' she said, producing a pair of horned-rim glasses from her designer clutch bag and putting them on.

I sat. Puzzled.

'It's my couch of contemplation, of meditation. Do you find it comfortable to sit on? Yes?'

'Yeah, very.' I sank into it and relaxed.

'Good. Now, in my spare time I have been studying psychiatry for several years. I am a great observer of human behaviour and I'm worried about you because I can see you have a stressful job and you're working far too hard.'

I went to speak and she held up her hand to silence me.

'No yapping! I get it, you're a small business with a lot of pressure to deliver results quickly. I understand what that feels like, believe me, but I have to ask how you are feeling, Harry. I am trained for this so don't worry. So first answer my questions are, do you feel a sense of disconnection from others, a feeling of being separate from people around you like you're an observer watching them through a two-way mirror?'

Obviously I did – it's what I used to do for a living.

'A little,' I said.

She smiled. 'Do you find yourself being cynical about everything and everyone?'

'Yeah.' I certainly did. There was a lot to be cynical about.

'I'll ask some more questions, nod your head if they apply. Do you feel tired and wired, by that I mean do you feel physically exhausted but still can't sleep? Do you skip meals and eat the wrong things late at night? Do you feel muddled and less sharp than you used to be?'

Mostly true but I gave every question a nod. Why not? I had to see where this was heading.

Maria leaned forward and half-whispered, 'Do you find it hard to feel pleasure?'

Again I nodded. This was getting odd. In the background Clair de Lune morphed into Air On The G String. Bach I think. She looked pensive.

'It's what I feared, Harry, you're on the verge of burnout. Complete and utter burnout. But it's not too late. Do you have healthcare?'

'I have the NHS…'

'Whatever. That's back home. You need help now, and that's where I come in. Remember I am psychiatrically trained and I know what I'm doing. So I want you to close your eyes, breathe in and out deeply, and let your mind empty. Try not to think at all. Do it, breathe in, hold it, then breathe out, in and out, deep breaths… do you feel the pressure flowing away?'

'Yeah.' I did actually.

'Good. Now keeping your eyes closed, think of something that would make you happy.'

She had moved closer to me, the light flowery smell of her Acqua Di Parma perfume had become stronger. She was inches away from me, her face hovering over mine. And then she kissed me, deeply and slowly, for what seemed like minutes, her right hand caressing my chest.

'Is that what you were thinking of?'

'Yes.'

'Good. Now keeping your eyes closed, think of something else that would give you great pleasure.'

She didn't give me much thinking time. Her hand dropped, and she ran her fingers up and down my inner thigh, getting closer to my mounting joy but never quite touching it.

She stopped abruptly, gave me a small kiss, and then she slowly ran a fingernail up and down her target until it threatened to burst through the fabric of my jeans.

'We'd better give that some air, mister,' she said.

Maria unzipped my flies gently and guiding little Harry into the light. I didn't even attempt to resist. I just made a quick deal with my conscience – I would happily succumb to the coming suck-come, but that would be the end of it. Nothing more, I promised myself. Nothing more… Probably.

I felt her tongue start to tease its way around me, darting and flicking and then....

Bang! Bang! Bang! Someone was knocking on the cellar door, heavily and repeatedly.

Maria quickly straightened herself out and went up the stairs to answer it as I forced myself into an approximation of decency.

I heard Andre's voice. 'Maria! I need Harry to come up here now.'

I started climbing the stairs. 'Where's the fire?'

He was looking at me and ignoring Maria.

'Harry, clam up, and follow me. We need to get out of this place now.'

'Leave? I...'

'Seriously, shut the fuck up, put your head down and follow me.'

I did what I was told. Head down, eyes on him, through the bar... We were out on the pavement about fifteen seconds later.

'What's happening?'

'The bar. It's a trap. It's filling up with dodgy geezers, the two that were there before and others who look a lot like them. It feels like they're waiting for someone, but they are definitely hostile, man. If looks could kill I'd be an extra on Six Feet Under. We have to get away, pronto.'

'Okay, let's shoot.'

'We'll take the subway from Sutphin Boulevard, get off at Lexington, and hail a cab.'

'Okay.'

We started walking. The sun was setting, but it was still light. Andre was giving me the stink eye.

'So what was that about, don't tell me you were giving her a tip?'

'Your mind! No. I might have been about to give her a deposit.'

'Sick, you know... do you even remember what we talked about? This woman was or most likely is the wife

132

of a high-ranking mobster yet but you're down there happily contemplating slipping her the baloney pony!'

'Guilty as charged!'

He laughed. 'You fuckin' idiot. You wanted to schtupp when we needed to schlepp.'

I grabbed his arm. 'Andre, look up there to your left, the Age of Aquarius is back.'

Our old friends in the yellow VW campervan were parked about twenty feet down the street with the engine ticking over. The driver, a miniature Hagrid with a mess of greying hair and haystack whiskers, spotted us immediately. He revved up and headed straight towards us. The front seat passenger, a fiercely cropped dark-haired woman, leaned out of the window and trained an antique pistol on us. It was old, it looked like a 19th century Deringer but it worked. Two shots rang out, and they weren't frighteners. If the gunwoman had been proficient, and had she been wielding a weapon manufacture this side of World War II we would have been in serious trouble.

***

Sir Timothy Storey looked slightly worried. He was in the back of his chauffeur-driven limp en route to Heathrow with just a carry-on bag – a few of his favourite casual clothes, the best New Bond Street had to offer, packed into a brown leather Hermes cabin suitcase. But the man in his ear was relentless.

Although he was keeping his voice as calm as a summer fishpond the conversation was making Sir Tim ever so slightly rattled.

'Yes, I understand that things are getting frightfully out of hand, Guilio,' he said with as much patience as he could muster. 'I'm on my way over now. We have to conclude this tonight, tie up all of the loose ends and make sure the business is not affected by any of this.

Please, please ensure that bloodshed is kept to a minimum.'

The phone crackled with an angry expletive-heavy response from the caller. Tim offered a few more placations then ended the one-sided conversation.

'Fuckin' dumb wop,' he snarled in an accent that would have turned heads at his alma mater, Eton College, for all the wrong reasons.

He opened his wallet, looked at the picture of Amelia inside, and sighed. She used to be so sweet. What use was she to him now? Just a nuisance. An itch he can't scratch. She would have to go.

Still a few days in New York restructuring the businesses would cheer him up. At least he'd have time to visit a few Frank Lloyd Wright buildings in the tri-state area and sample the delight of some unspoilt Mexican peaches.

***

I grabbed hold of Andre and started running back down the street towards the restaurant. My plan was to run past it and take a left but the hippy VW had mounted the pavement behind us. We had no choice but to burst back into the bar area.

***

Chapter 10

Inside Santa Monica Steakhouse, the large lumbering man known only as The Ox opened the metal door and looked at Amelia Storey. She was bound and gagged. The way he preferred women to be. The Ox was not a bright or cultured man. In the middle of sentencing him, a judge had once referred to him as a 'sentient blob' – a description so accurate that even his colleagues in Boston referred to him as the SB. He didn't mind. He thought it stood for Son-of-a Bitch. Not a bright man.

The old eaterie on West 49th Street had long been closed-down, after the NYC Health Department eventually lost patience with the owner's vague notion of what constituted a pristine restaurant environment. To passers-by, the building looked dead. Its frontage was boarded up, with signs screaming 'Danger! No entry! Building awaiting demolition!' plastered all over it. The only way in was through the back of the building, down a service alley that was lightless at night and unsettling by day.

The only noise he could hear was emanating from the walk-in cold storage unit, where he was now standing. It was buzzing away gently accompanied by Storey's light snoring. The broad was still out cold – those roofies work wonders, he thought. Even at this temperature, with her clothes dirty and torn, she still looked hot.

The Ox had been tempted when he had first thrown her on the filthy old mattress. Very tempted. It would have been over in a couple of lust-fuelled minutes. If that. But then he had thought better of it. Kevin had made it clear that she was important and was to come to no unnecessary harm, or he would face retribution from on high.

Even a simpleton like The Ox knew what that meant. He rolled the pretty girl on her back. She'd lost a bit of blood judging by the stain on her t-shirt. He rolled it up and looked at the deep cut under her left breast. He'd have to get young Johnny Linden over to patch that up.

The Ox dropped into a squat, not easy with his aching knees, to roll her t-shirt back down. But then changed his mind, roughly jerking her bra up and above her generous breasts. He let out a low whistle as he savoured the view. They were the finest tits he'd ever seen in the flesh. Instinctively, his hand reached for his flies. Jerking off wasn't hurting her, he figured.

***

Johnny Baby and Giuliano sat at the back of the small café in Mulberry Street. Johnny looked around the room with a slight sense of guilt and allowed faded memories of good times to flood his mind. With its dark wooden walls, round mirrors and signed pictures of old stars – Sinatra, Frankie Valli, Tony Bennett, Monica Vitti – Guiseppe's always reminded him of growing up, of being young, hunting with the pack and having the world at his feet.

He didn't get back here as much as he would have liked to and the look of surprise on old man Stefano's face when he walked in had almost shamed him. Especially when it turned to joy and warm embraces. Stefano had known his father and his grandfather from the old country.

Back in the 70s, Johnny and his crew were always holed up here, working out new schemes to make a buck and discussing who was next to be on the receiving end of their brand of radical entrepreneurship. Protection money was always a good bet. They drank coffee after coffee and laughed and ripped the shit out of each other while Bruce Springsteen and Billy Joel played endlessly on the jukebox. The Boss and The Piano Man, Mr Long Island. His kind of rock music.

Pretty much nothing had changed in here except for him. He felt a different person entirely. Certainly a more tired one. He was exhausted and exasperated by his bellicose brother-in-law who sat opposite pinching his nose and sniffing. What a lost cause.

Giuliano had no such fond memories. One old café was pretty much the same as another. The past was the past so fuck it! He only had his eyes on the future and being dragged to some nostalgic shithole in Little Italy by his temporary boss was just another obstacle in his way.

'This kidnapping in the village. What have you heard?' Johnny said quietly.

'What kidnapping?'

'C'mon. You musta heard. A punk chick working at the soup kitchen. Snatched on the street outside. What's the word?'

'What the fuck's that got to do with us?' His breakfast coke was making him bolder.

Johnny snarled. 'I got people that are interested, that's what the fuck it's got to do with us.'

Guilio, realising his attitude was rattling Infantino, adopted a straighter face and a more conciliatory tone.

'I ain't heard shit, Johnny. Not a word. What about your cops? They gotta know something, am I right?'

'They got their own problems,' Johnny replied bluntly.

He looked away, staring at the distant hustle and bustle outside the faded shopfront window.

'Do me a personal favour, have your guys ask around and find out what you can. I don't like this shit. There's something brewing, and it's disrupting our plans.'

'I will boss. Maybe it's BMB or Milla Bloods, the gangs. They got no respect.'

Johnny grunted. Giuliano didn't move.

'So move! Get on it now! I haven't come this far to spend the last of my days rotting in Attica on some mother-fucking RICO charge. I got my family to think of.'

Giulio stood up and stormed off, letting the door slam behind him. Johnny sighed and took his hand off the gun that was resting on his thigh.

The bill was still on the table. $18. The lousy bum hadn't paid it. All his money was going up his schnoz. He put the pistol in his shoulder holster and left a $50 dollar bill on top of it.

Stefano walked over nervously.

'Mr Infantino,' he said hesitantly. 'Is he okay?'

'Why do you ask, my friend?'

'May I speak openly?'

'Of course, *ovviamente*.'

'Signore Clarini, he's upsetting people. People he shouldn't be upsetting.'

Johnny smiled warmly. 'How so?'

'He went into a bar in Long Island a few nights ago, a bar run by friends, and caused trouble. My son-in-law is married to the owner's daughter, good people. Our people. Your Guiliani was taking drugs in public, cocaine, and would not stop when he was asked to.'

'What happened?'

'He and his rowdy friends laughed at them and demanded protection money. The bar is already protected.'

Johnny Baby nodded. Long Island was Lucchese territory.

'What happened?'

'When they refused to pay him, Clarini put a bar stool through the plate-glass window and one of his men, a big dumb idiota, stole wine. Clarini said they would be back. Obviously the owners are worried.'

Johnny breathed deeply and turned. He held his breath, then breathed out slowly as he studied the nearest painting on the wall for what seemed like minutes. The painting showed the Scala dei Turchi – the Turkish steps

– a rocky cliff on the coast of Realmonte near Porto Empedocle, southern Sicily. He'd visited it with his parents decades ago. Happy memories. Good times.

'Tell them not to be worried, Stefano,' he said finally. 'I will put a stop to this. Guiliani will pay for the repair.'

The old man looked visibly relieved. 'I am sorry if I have spoken out of turn.'

'No. Hai fatto bene. You've done the right thing. This idiocy could cause everybody problems.'

Johnny rose to his feet. 'Ciao Stefano,' he said. 'I'll be back soon, mio amico. Dio vi benedica.'

***

Andre was right. The bar was full of hostiles. I looked around. The customers had all gone. The only people left were Maria, Isabella, Chiara and now a total of six men who didn't appear to be Italian-American. Almost certainly they were Bostonians, clinging on to their distant Irish heritage. The first two, the scouts, were sitting with the women, another bigger man were sitting at the adjoining table, one guy was at the bar and the other two were closer to us.

One of them, with hooded eyes and curly hair, moved towards us. He had a blackjack in his hand. It was about eight inches long with a woven leather handle and a hefty knob at the end. There was no doubt that it would do a fair bit of damage.

I held up my hands as if surrendering, allowing him to come closer, and closer, until he was just close enough…

I threw a straight arm punch, and it was a good'un. My target was his Adam's apple. If he hadn't swerved to his left, my fist would have shattered his windpipe. Instead, it crashed into the right side of his jaw, so I followed through by smashing my elbow hard into the back of his head. One down, five to go. Two and a half each.

Now all the men were standing up. The guy at the bar had produced a handgun which he was currently aiming straight at me. His eyes were so fixed on me, I didn't think he could have noticed Andre moving towards him. The piece was an M1911 – I remember thinking it must have been an antique. That's when time slowed down. As I held my hands up in surrender, trying not to look at Andre, Chiara screamed, sprung out of her seat and raced towards me. Andre reached the gunman just as he was taking a shot, knocking his arm to one side. The sound of the gunshot was deafening but Andre's intervention meant the bullet hit Chiara not me.

I shouted 'No!' as I raced towards her and then the nearest guy to me swung his blackjack.

As they say in the old the best pulp fiction books, a black well opened up before my eyes and I dived in.

***

Johnny Linden arrived at the Santa Monica Steakhouse through the backdoor. The Ox led him awkwardly to the cold storage unit. Linden let the big bald giant shuffle in first. He didn't trust the man, nobody did, but he didn't dare antagonise him. The Ox grunted. The roofies must have worn off. Amelia was sitting on the edge of the mattress and had managed to loosen the ropes binding her arms, but not her gag.

When she saw them, she started to shout. An incomprehensible torrent of words flew at them.

'Easy, easy. I'm here to help,' said Linden, who was visibly shocked.

'Why is she being treated like this?' he said angrily.

The Ox shot him a look. 'Just fix the bitch. Unless you fancy joining her.'

Johnny knew better than to argue.

'Okay. Listen, I'm going to need hot water and a sponge or a clean flannel or at least some paper towels.'

The Ox didn't move.

'I am a doctor, please get me what I have asked for unless you want this poor girl to die on us.'

He wasn't a doctor – he'd dropped out of med school in his second year – and she wasn't in danger of dying. But Linden knew he had to assert some authority over the great clueless thug to help the girl get through this.

Whatever this was.

As The Ox lumbered out, Johnny looked around the room in despair. The mattress Amelia Storey was sitting on could easily have been rescued from a skip; the only other furniture was a piss bucket in the corner, as yet unused. The floor was concrete and bare except for the odd speck of blood and what looked disturbing like a serving spoon sized puddle of semen.

She tried to talk again. Johnny shook his head.

'I'm going to push you back to examine the wound,' he said gently. The girl nodded and laid back of her own accord. He pushed her t-shirt up and reached inside his medical kit-bag as the Ox came back in with the hot water and a box of tissues.

He looked at the woman's bare stomach and leered.

'That will be all,' snapped Linden. 'Leave us.' The Ox's lip curled but he didn't move.

'The infection! Dammit man! Cellulitis.'

The Ox left as quickly as his ailing joints allowed, retreating to a dirty Formica table outside covered with playing cards. Not normal cards of course. His were adorned with topless women.

Linden looked at Amelia. Her eyes were smiling.

'Cellulitis,' he repeated almost under his breath. 'I had to say something to get rid of the big lug. I knew he wouldn't understand it. Now, I'm just going to give you a local anaesthetic and sew this up, okay.'

The woman nodded. This one wasn't so bad.

***

I was aware of a streetlight shining through the blinds, the sound of people talking in whispers, and a pain in my head that didn't feel like a hangover.

Where was I?

I squinted at the walls without moving. No décor, just paint. I didn't know the room, but I recognised Maria's voice. I turned over slowly, Andre was spark out next to me alongside a woman with her back to me who was clearly in the same state. Maria and Isabella were with Chiara who had been bleeding heavily. Nobody else was in the room.

'How is she?' I crocked.

'She'll live,' said Maria. 'The bullet missed her heart by an inch and passed through her upper chest. I've used the first aid kit to patch her but we need to get her to hospital. I've given her OxyCotin for pain control.'

'Good thinking. And who's that lying next to Andre?'

Maria shook her head. 'Some dame who burst into the restaurant just after they coshed you. She had a gun in her hands so they coshed her too.'

I nodded and walked over. It was Sammy the butch woman from the soup kitchen. It must have been her riding shotgun in the hippy bus. She looked younger and more feminine without the snarl. I still liked her hairstyle – skinhead girl style at the front, razor-cut at the back.

She had good cheekbones, and she was dressed in leather and denim with heavy silver rings on every knuckle.

They had inscriptions, but I was too far away to read them. The room we were in was pretty bare. Just a white settee – yeah, another one – and a lot of stacked boxes of rice and pasta. I spotted a small handsaw lodged between the boxes and a bottle of Roccolo Grassi on the floor. The top of the bottle was smothered in melted candle wax and the remains of a candle poked from the mouth. There was a mattress in the corner and next to that was an empty bucket – presumably the toilet facility.

Small untidy piles of ciabatta rolls had been left on dinner plates, all of which suggested our captors hadn't been planning on initiating a hostage situation but had stumbled into it and were keeping us alive for now, presumably as bargaining chips.

There was nothing else in the room.

'Where are we?'

'Upstairs.'

I looked over at Maria.

'Is this minimalism or can't you afford furniture?'

She laughed. 'It was the storage room but we were turning it into an admin office. They moved a lot of things out in a hurry including the desk and the chairs.'

Made sense. The chairs could have been broken up and used as weapons, but it was careless to have left the bottle and the saw.

The dinner plates looked quite solid too. Not much use against handguns though.

Andre groaned.

'Wakey wakey pard'ner.'

'Where are we?'

'Same shit, different landing. We're upstairs.'

'And the Irish?'

'Downstairs,' said Maria. 'They're Boston, led by Kevin Malone who is down there running the shit-show.'

'Do they know who you are?' I asked pointedly.

'They do now,' she replied.

'Who's she?' Andre asked of the comatose woman.

'Your stalker.'

'Samantha?'

'Yeah. She looks a bit like Emma Frost with a haircut. Same cheekbones.'

'Who's Em…'

Outside a convoy of vehicles pulled up abruptly.

'More shit,' muttered Maria.

***

Downstairs, the restaurant phone rang. Malone, looking grimmer than usual, answered it abruptly.

'We're closed.'

'It's me,' growled the man at the other end of the line who was wearing a Rolex Oyster and a $30,000 diamond encrusted gold bracelet.

'Giulio…'

'You dumb-fuck Mick. Do you know where you are?'

Malone said nothing, assuming correctly that it was a rhetorical question and more intemperate abuse was on the way.

'You've got Johnny Baby's wife, you've got my fucking wife and you've got Johnny's daughter…'

Malone's long grey face seemed to turn longer and wearier as he listened. Better keep the bad news coming.

'And we've got company outside, G. Heavy company. Famigilia…'

'Johnny knows? Shit. The cops must have tipped him off.'

'He's sent the cavalry.'

'Yeah it's Wounded Knee and you're the fuckin' Lakota tribe.'

Malone scratched absentmindedly at his fuzzy five o'clock shadow, plucking up the courage to ask.

'Can you do anything?' he said, finally.

'Can I do anything? *Che pallo!* At what fucking point did I tell you to kidnap my fucking family?'

'It was a mistake, G. My guys just trailed the bald prick here, like you asked, they didn't know who owned the joint.'

'How many are outside?'

'Brendan, how many are outside?'

'Three cars, twelve men.'

'He says twelve of them. There's five of us.'

Giuliani thought quickly. 'We need to make this look like an ongoing hostage situation. Sit tight and barricade the doors. I'll phone Mick Quinn. No wait, first you ring the number I'm going to text to you and get them to tell Mr Infantino that his wife and daughter will be released once $100,000 have been transferred to an offshore account, I will also have those details texted to you.'

'Who shall I say we are?'

Giulio smiled. 'Tell them you're the Hazelwood Mob from Pittsburgh, and tell them you also want Antonio Guerrero released from prison.'

'Who's he?'

'One of the Cuban Five from Miami. Just to confuse the fuckers.'

Both men laughed. Might as well sting the bastard a little bit more before he loses his crown.

Malone put the phone down and allowed himself to crack a graveyard smile. It was all going to be cool.

***

Detective Inspector Michael 'Mick' Quinn took Giulio's call, made a mental note of the sum he was promised, and physical notes about the hostage situation and the hefty ransom demand. He informed First Deputy Commissioner Frank Garvey that an armed siege was in progress in Queens with hostages and got the go ahead to intervene, over-riding any local police involvement. Seventeen minutes later he pulled up outside the restaurant with four squad cars; the hostage negotiator arrived ten minutes later by which time the twelve Mafiosi loyal to Infantino had made a tactical retreat.

***

Things weren't looking good for Chiara. Maria had stemmed the blood flow temporarily but the bullet wound seemed to have a life of its own, pulsing and pumping a little more claret down Chiara's chest with each beat.

As Maria soldiered on, using everything she could find to stop the flow, Isabella flopped down onto the settee in tears and started reciting what must have been a prayer in Italian.

'O Signore, guarisci il nostro caro Amelia e Chiara, e dona a loro la forza di sopportare la malattia con pazienza. Ti preghiamo di concedergle la salute e la tua benedizione. Amen.'

She crossed herself and sobbed. I looked at Andre and nodded towards the room's one small window. It opened from the inside but was securely barred. There was no way through it without bolt covers. He walked over.

'Did you ever feel the fabric of your life was coming unspun?' I said softly.

'Eh?'

'This job, mate, it should have been so easy. Find the girl, have a ball, go home.'

'Aye. And look at us now. Banged up, as you'd say, and held prisoner for no apparent reason by a bunch of homicidal Mick maniacs…'

***

Downstairs, the Boston boys stood in a loose arc close to the bar. Kevin Malone did his best to maintain an air of sombre funeral director authority.

'You two barricade both doors, and Brendan, you keep the Feds under surveillance. The fuckin' idiots have saved our bacon. They won't make a move while we've got the hostages but we need to expedite this process. We'll get the women out of here as soon as we can. The private dicks could be a problem but remember they are expendable. Very expendable. Nobody will care if they are collateral damage, do you get me?'

'Why the fuck did we stick them up there in the first place?' said Matt Kelly. If he sounded impatient, it was because he was. In his spare time, he drummed with a thriving Celtic folk band and was due on stage at 10pm.

'Who gives a fuck?' snapped Malone, fully aware that his leadership qualities were being questioned by the whole crew. 'They're up there now, and as soon as the money is transferred, the women will walk and we'll be on our way.'

'Have you asked for a helicopter?' asked Jack Cleery.

'Why the fuck would I do that, Jack?' snapped Malone, clearly exasperated.

'It's what they do in all the hostage movies.'

Malone sighed. 'Where the fuck is it going to land, you meathead? Out the back on top of the bins and beer barrels? On the street through the overhead power lines and the fucking phone wires? Or shall I ask for an amphibious fucker that can float down East River, maybe with a flotilla of currachs from the auld country, and take off from the water?'

'Kev!' Big Brendan O'Reilly called out from the window.

"What already?!'

'A car-loads of wops just drove past.'

'Our friends from Jersey?'

'No. They look like Infantino's crew again checking out the numbers.'

'Jesus.'

'And a TV crew just showed up. ABC7 Eyewitness News. Fox 5 won't be far behind.'

Malone's face turned from grey to red. He pointed over at some tables near the back of the room and yelled at his men.

'Get them against the door now. And everyone except Big Brendan stay away from the windows! Use the tables to create defensive positions just in case anyone feels the need to storm in.'

The next hour would be crucial, he thought. Quinn was cool, but TV coverage would most likely increase the chances of him being replaced by someone senior. They had to get a wriggle on or this whole thing would go arseways.

***

The Ox had lurched out of the Santa Monica Steakhouse for his 'evening break' – which she knew by the smell of his breath when he returned would mean beer, fries, burgers, more fries, and possibly paid-for affection. She had an hour, maybe more.

Johnny Linden came in to check on her, almost immediately. She started shaking.

'Amelia, you okay?'

She mumbled through the gag, wriggling, and pleading with her eyes. It worked. He took it off.

'Thank you. I was having some kind of panic attack. The gag, the fear, being tied up… I'm claustrophobic at the best of times, and germophobic, so this situation is as close to hell as I've ever been.'

He looked sympathetic. Mug. She hesitated and continued, 'God knows what my father will say…'

She looked away, but she knew that throwaway line would have registered. She turned on the waterworks with long practiced ease.

'Hey, nothing's going to happen to you.' Linden put his arm around her, to comfort her. 'Why don't I take you through to the other room while the Ox is out? You can use the restaurant washroom and walk around a bit. I'll untie you. Obviously, I trust you. Come on, I don't think you're no risk to me.'

Bingo. 'Of course I'm not. Thank you Johnny, thank you. You're my knight in shining armour.'

He undid the lock on her chain, helped her up and led her through to the restaurant area.

'It's pretty grim out here too, but at least you can sit at the table or walk around. Here, I'll take you to the powder room.'

As they stopped outside the Ladies, she looked deep into his eyes as if she were planning on kissing him and instead unleashed a *sanbon-zuki* – a savage three punch combo.

She smiled. Years of karate training and the black belt had not been wasted.

A sudden sound behind her made her spin around…

It was getting noisier outside. I stepped over to the window and looked out through the bars.

'There are cops out there now, and camera crews.'

'Let me see.'

I moved so Andre could survey the activity.

'That's Micky Quinn.'

'Good guy?'

'I think he might be sideways, bent y'know.'

'You don't say.'

'Buster would know, but…

'But no phones so no way to ask. We need answers mate, and lots of them.'

Over on the floor Chiara gave a low moan. I nodded slightly towards her.

'We need to sort this out pronto, Tonto. She ain't gonna last long.'

He grimaced. I grabbed him by the arms.

'What the fuck is this all about?'

'I'm really not sure H. Sometimes you find yourself in one of those moments when you realise life can only be understood backwards, even though it must be lived forwards.'

'For fuck's sake! You're misquoting Kierkegaard at me? Jesus.' My tone hardened. 'Andre, I love you likely an annoying brother but if you know something – anything – more about the shit-storm that we've landed in, now would be a good time to speak up. Why are a bunch of Boston bogtrotters kidnapping Mob family members? I can't think of many things riskier. I mean, Johnny Baby's wife? Fuckin' hell! I'd rather kick Scott Summers in the balls and pull off his visor. It's like they're trying to call on a full-on gang war, but why would they do that?'

Andre's face contorted. It looked like he wanted to say something and was battling himself. Angel on one shoulder, devil on the other style. Instead he ignored my question and changed the subject.

'One of the Irish is outside guarding the door. Let's see what he has to say.'

I nodded, but I wasn't happy. My niggling doubts about my old buddy were mounting.

'He'll say nothing unless we make him,' I said finally. 'Give me a minute.'

The window had a heavy, old-fashioned casing around it. I started tugging at the corner and broke off a length. It snapped off cleanly, but the crack echoed around the room. I paused and stayed silent. There was no response from the guard outside. Not a movement, not a dicky bird. But the casing was too light for the job I had in mind.

A low groan distracted me. The Butch woman also known as Sammy had come to, and was taking in the surroundings.

Andre spoke first. 'Lady, speaking as someone who recently tried to kill me, have we got a problem here?'

'Are you the guys who kidnapped Amelia?'

'No they're not,' said Maria. 'They're the guys trying to keep us and Chiara safe from the bozos downstairs.'

Samantha Evison looked at her and Chiara, taking in the situation.

'Amelia,' she groaned, obviously still confused.

'Who told you we had kidnapped Amelia?'

'Jason.'

'Tippy Jay?'

'Yeah.'

'For fuck's sake. We don't know who the kidnappers are or if they're connected to the Boston mob downstairs, but we do know we need to get out of here a-sap.'

She nodded. I helped Sammy to her feet, gave her the old wine bottle and told her what to do. The plan was improvised and unsubtle, but stranger things and all that.

I nodded to Andre that we were ready.

'Hey,' he shouted through the door. 'This chick in here is dying, man. We need some hot water to change her dressing.'

By nature, Patrick McEvoy was not a people person, but today his hangover served only to amplify his sociopathic tendencies.

'Go fuck yourself,' he barked.

I went to say something but Andre held his finger up and shook his head.

'Come on, man. I know this wasn't what you planned. Don't add negligent homicide to the list of crimes you'll be charged with. You wouldn't want to be responsible for the death of Giuliano Clarini's daughter, would you? If the Feds don't get you, Giulio will – and you know how that'll pan out. You might as well eat your gun now and save yourself a world of hurt.'

Nothing.

'Come on, pal. Just some hot water, that's all we need to keep the poor kid alive.'

Andre paused. There was a moment of silence and then we heard the guy walk away from the door and down the creaking stairs to the restaurant kitchen.

'It worked,' I said.

'I figured self-preservation would trump compassion.'

'Now for the hard part, mate.'

We got into position and waited.

'Do you think we'll make the New York Post?' I asked, killing time. 'I always liked that paper.'

'You mean Page Six or the news pages – 'Headless body in topless bar gives tough guy Tyler the finger'?'

'Yeah, that's what I'm talking about. A beaut. That sort of thing. Let's find ourselves a topless bar once this is all over.'

Sammy tutted loudly and the kitchen stairs started to creak.

'Sssh. He's coming back… wait…listen… yeah, he's on his own.'

'Let's hope he don't spill the water.'

I raised my eyebrows at Andre and we both took a deep breath.

'Stand back,' barked Patrick.

The lock clicked open, and the door opened slightly. He could see that both of us had stepped back. He had the bowl of water, which meant his gun was either tucked into the back of his strides or was parked safely in his shoulder holster. He motioned for us to go back even further, then stepped forward and slowly lowered the bowl of water.

As soon as it was on the floor, Sammy stepped from behind the door and whacked him hard with the wine bottle, which shattered all over the carpet. He fell flat on his face with a loud thump and I followed through with a size ten boot to the head – just to guarantee he was out for the count.

Someone shouted 'Pat?' from the bottom of the stairs. Then footsteps started coming up them. Andre moved quickly, grabbing the key from the outside the keyhole, then slamming the door shut and locking it.

Now we had a hostage of our own.

I looked at Sammy. She was crying.

'You okay, luv?'

'I cut his head open.'

'He's a bad guy, you're allowed.'

She sobbed louder. She had nice eyes. Unusual colour. Kind of gold green. They were welling up with tears.

I feigned indignity. 'Hey, you were trying to *shoot* me.'

'I was trying to scare you, to make you surrender and lead us to where we thought you had Amelia tucked away.'

'Where did you get that squirrel gun? The frigging Antiques Roadshow?'

She laughed. 'It was my grandad's.'

I offered her a hug which she accepted.

'We will find Amelia, Sammy, and we will save Amelia, together, okay?'

She looked confused but said nothing. I carried on. 'And if any more bad guys get in your way, you have Lord Timothy Storey's permission to hurt them with anything in your vicinity.'

She smiled. 'He sounds important.'

'He's rich. It's not the same thing.'

***

Deputy Commissioner Frank Garvey was already at home in bed, the worst for wear after a long lunch, when he was disturbed by the low buzz of the mobile phone in his bedside cabinet. This was his private number, only to be used in cases of dire emergences and with his puffed-up sense of self-importance he was furious that it was being used at all.

'Who is this?' he demanded in a hushed tone as his wife stirred restlessly in the bed beside him.

'It's Buster. Are you out of your mind sending Quinn to deal with a hostage situation way off his patch?'

'What I choose to do or not do is entirely at my discretion Campbell,' hissed Garvey. 'How dare you call me on this number? I'll have you seeing out your career teaching road safety to school kids for this.'

'I don't think so,' said Buster with a confidence that immediately unsettled Garvey. 'I got a box today from some interested parties. Very interesting. Lots of pictures, lots of tapes, surveillance reports. A whole lot of trouble for some of the finest... and the rest.'

'What are you insinuating Campbell? If you have evidence, you should submit it.'

'All of it?' said Buster as if he was playing with a fish on a hook. 'There seem to be some nice places around town. Places I've never been. Not on my salary. Eleven

Madison Park, Jean Georges, The River Café... all top joints I'd imagine?'

Garvey sighed and his shoulders drooped.

'What do you want Buster?'

'I know we can't sort out the whole department, but I want my precinct and the 7th spring cleaned – and I want to do it. I'm not living in a dreamworld, but this would be a start. Broken windows theory in practice Frank. Your old friend Rudy would be proud of you.'

'And the rest?' said Garvey with a sigh of resignation.

'Once the job's done, all that shit will disappear Frank. That's all I want. We go way back. I don't want to rock your boat.'

Garvey sighed. Defeated but re-assured. Buster Campbell might be the world's biggest pain in the butt, but he was also a man of his word.

'Okay, okay, I'll make some calls. You're taking this operation over. Get to work but keep it clean.'

'Cleaner than the board of health baby,' laughed Buster down the line.

***

'Kevin!' shouted Declan McCann as he burst back down into the bar, red-faced and panting.

'What? What the fuck?' snapped Malone whose patience was now as stretched as spandex pants on an over-fed buffalo.'

'They've got Pat.'

'Who have?'

'Those two dicks and the dames. I heard a noise upstairs. I went up and he's gone. They must have grabbed him.'

Malone went silent and took a long, ragged inward breath as he shook his head slowly.

'That stupid motherfucker was meant to be keeping them locked in. How the fuck did they get him inside?'

It was a rhetorical question but it would be fair to say that Declan McCann's Mensa membership would not be arriving by FedEx any day soon.

'He must have opened the door,' he said, beaming as if he was helping to solve the mystery of life.

Malone slapped him hard across the cheek and then grabbed him in a headlock.

'Are you fucking with me? Are you?'

'I'm sorry boss, Jeez, I'm sorry. Stop man, stop.'

Malone released his grip. 'Declan, you fuck off upstairs and keep guard outside the room. Everybody just sit tight, all right? No shooting, no yacking, no jerking off and no opening any fucking doors! I will fix this.'

The crew exchanged glances but nobody said a word. Malone knew they had doubts, but hey, so did he. Turning his back on them, he crossed himself quickly. There was the only way this escalating clusterfuck could have a happy ending. Divine intervention.

***

'Is much going on out there?' I asked.

'Nothing. Quinn is just sitting there. It's more a case of police meditation than attempted mediation.'

'A delaying tactic?'

'Maybe. But why?'

***

It was the Ox. He'd come back unexpectedly early. He was standing there with half of a foot-long Subway sandwich in his hand and a trickle of ketchup on his chin. He was big, but he was also fat and slow. She could take him.

She adopted a *Heiko dachi* ready stance. He shook his head and pulled out a Rhino 50DS.

'On your knees,' he barked. She shrugged and complied. He walked behind her, keeping out of range of possible kicks. Then he stopped for a moment, crunched down on the sandwich and knocked her unconscious with the pistol butt.

Bosh! Out went the lights.

The Ox sighed. He'd liked it here, but the Englishman had arrived and it was time to go.

***

Patrick McEvoy regained consciousness to find that his left arm was tied to a radiator with some torn fabric and his right arm was strapped to the top of a wooden crate. That didn't look good. The bald prick stood beside him holding the small saw, which looked worse.

'What the fuck is going on?'

I smiled. 'Now listen mate, we've got a bit of a situation here and we need a few answers.'

Patrick's lip curled as he prepared to deliver some stock insult or defiant comeback. I raised a hand as if pleading for silence.

'Now I know you're busting to tell us something about our mothers or our wives or both but we don't have time for that macho bullshit. This young girl on the floor is in a very bad way so we need to find out what's happening here fast, and bring it to some kind of conclusion as quickly as possible.'

'Fuck yer ma,' he spat defiantly.

I gave Andre a hopeless shrug of my shoulders and then moved behind the moron and slammed my knee hard into his liver. McEvoy screamed, but I managed to suppress most of the racket by slapping my hand down across his mouth.

'Do you hear that, Paddy?' I said to him as he started to whimper. There was silence. 'Do you know what that is?' He shook his head slightly. 'That's the sound of your mates doing fuck all to help you out up here, so you'd better start talking, all right, and telling us what we need to know because believe me, we are your only chance of getting out of this mess alive.'

Patrick grimaced and then dropped his head in shame.

'What's this all about, buddy?' said Andre softly but firmly – the good cop to my bad cop. 'Why the fuck have you got us and the women holed in up here?'

'You're insurance,' McEvoy gasped as the pain subsided just enough for him to catch his breath. 'Well they are.' He nodded over at the woman.

'Insurance for what?' growled Andre, who was stroking the top of the broken bottle in a passable imitation of Blofeld and his Persian cat. This seemed to unsettle Patrick more than my bad cop roleplay.

I've seen this a lot. The guy might have the muscles, the ink and gym-built chest but, odds on, under pressure he was going to fold faster than a Chinese laundry.

Patrick twisted and pulled but his hands remained secured.

'You'd better start talking, mate,' said Andre in an even tone. 'For your own good. The longer he waits, the angrier my English friend gets.'

***

Outside of Silvio's, Detective Quinn and his men were not minded to take any risks to life and limb. There would be no heroic hostage rescue today, no daring-do, no men in Kevlar body arming smashing through doors and crashing through windows. Quinn's job was to contain the situation until told otherwise. He wasn't happy with the news crews spewing out their acres of wild speculation but there was little he could do but move them down the street apace for their own "protection". This was America after all, the story was live, and witnesses abounded. Local rubberneckers had joined the throng, and wild speculation about what was going on inside spread through the crowd like wildfire, which meant Twitter was abuzz, and that time was very much against them.

Pat McEvoy had plenty to say once he understood the situation.

'This wasn't supposed to happen. Believe me. This is a mess we're trying to get out of,' he said, speaking quickly and gruffly.

'So tell me who are you exactly, who are the mob downstairs.'

'Patrick McEvoy out of Worcester. We're the Malone boys. Boston, Boston Irish.'

'And you're here because?'

'Because we've been paid to be here. We're working for a local man.'

'Don't be shy, who hired you.'

He hesitated.

'C'mon.'

'Giuliano Clarini, we've been trailing you from the start.'

'You've been trailing me? What, in the sedan with the Twisted Sister sticker?'

'Yeah.'

'But that's out of Jersey.'

'Yes, so we wouldn't have Boston plates. Guilio has ties with the Jersey mob, they're doing him a favour.'

'And what price would they be charging for that?'

'I don't rightly know. But we also snatched the girl for him.'

'Boston took Amelia? For Guilio? Why?'

'It's some family shit. They didn't join the dots.'

'Is she still alive?'

'As far as I know. Guilio's partner is flying in to deal with the shit.'

I paused for thought. 'So Guilio had Boston nab his own niece, who is somehow related to Johnny Baby, for reasons unknown…'

I was baffled. Out of the corner of my eye I saw Chiara and Sammy exchange glances. Then Chiara shook her head, the universal sign for 'Shut it!'. But why?

'There's something bigger going on here,' said Andre.

'Yeah, but what?'

'We've been kept in the dark,' said McEvoy. 'We're just mercenaries in this.'

'It could be a power play. Johnny's been robbed, his family are at risk, he'll be chewing the carpet. Sew enough confusion and make a move…'

'And the women were needed as bargaining chips in case anything went tits up.'

I looked at Pat McEvoy. 'If your boys snatched Amelia, you must know where she is.'

'Yeah, yeah. She's at the Santa Monica Steakhouse with The Ox. But listen. It's coming to a head tonight. Johnny's gonna get wiped out.'

'Leaving Guilio in charge,' said Andre.

'It's the only thing that makes sense.'

'Jersey could be his back-up. He moves into the vacuum left by Johnny's demise and Malone's mob get a sweet deal down the line.'

I gave McEvoy the stink-eye. 'So some of your lot, Giuliano and some fucking Jersey boys are putting all this in motion?' I shook my head in disbelief. 'Nah, it don't add up.'

'It's true, I swear. There's probably more to it, but that's all I know.'

I looked at the women. They had said nothing for some time. Either they knew what was going down, or this is a complete surprise for them all.

'It's true, it's true,' screamed McEvoy. 'That Jersey crew are hard core and some big time English money man is pulling the strings. He's the one flying in.'

'Sir Tim,' I said almost to myself.

'You know it brother.'

That was it. Being barricaded in a room, battered, tired and somehow caught up in a tangle between two or three serious criminal firms was bad enough but knowing I'd was being fucked with got right on my thru'pennies.

'So why the fuck did he bring me over here in the first place?'

'That's my fault,' gasped Chiara weakly but this time her accent was pure cut-glass English. 'I'm Amelia.'

***

The dim light in the Santa Monica Steakhouse was starting to unsettle the Ox. Johnny was still unconscious, the bitch was back on her mattress, and he was on his own, playing with his dick. He puffed heavily on a thick blunt, drawing the acrid smoke deep into his lungs, and then prodded away at his mobile phone, growing increasingly fretful. Malone. Patrick. Declan. No answer from any of the motherfuckers.

He knew tonight was the night and even his low-watt brain power registered that something was wrong.

He walked awkwardly over and opened the cold store door a crack to peer at the girl. She didn't seem to be breathing. Flat on her back with her arms lying lifelessly by her side.

Just like sleeping beauty.

He thought about creeping in and touching her once more but he suddenly felt a wave of fear overcome him. He shut the door quietly and then he left the building.

***

'You're Amelia?' Andre spoke for all of us. Except the older women who exhibited no surprise.

They had known! Of course they had!

'I am,' she replied weakly. 'I will explain… everything, but…'

'But what matters is getting you to hospital, getting you out of here,' I said. 'Any ideas?'

'Is there any way out of here from this level without using the kitchen stairs?' asked Andre.

'There's a window that isn't barred out the door and to the left, but you'd be looking at a drop of maybe ten feet,' said Maria.

'There are bins there though,' Isabella added.

Andre beamed. 'Winner, winner, chicken dinner, we can do this, we've just got to get past that jerk on the door.'

'And then face Quinn, who may be on the take.'

***

Micky Quinn watched the black and whites driving towards Silvio's and scratched his head as they pulled up on the edge of the crowd. He wasn't expecting reinforcements, and he certainly wasn't expecting that uptight prick Buster Campbell to exit the first car with a team behind him, all coming his way.

'Hey, Prince, how's it hanging? You here to learn how real cops operate?'

Buster laughed. 'In a way, DI Quinn. These officers are from Internal Affairs. You're leaving now. With them. This investigation had been authorised by Deputy Commissioner Garvey. Send your boys back to the precinct. The real cops are in charge now.'

***

'Something's happening out there,' Andre said, looking out the window.

'Can you see who it is?'

'More cars, more cops.'

'Maybe it's the boys for the NYPD choir come to sing us Galway Bay.

'Hold on, I can see Buster down there.'

'On his Todd?'

'Firm-handed. Looks like he's sending Quinn and his boys away. Quinn is in the back of a black and white.'

'Let me see.' I squeezed past him. 'Result. So now we can get out knowing there are no hostiles outside the building.'

'Harry, Sammy, with me, ladies follow when it's safe.'

Andre opened the door quietly, expecting to face Declan Murphy. Fate was on our side. He was there, but he had his back to us as he listened to the growing babble of conversation downstairs. The Boston boys had obviously seen Quinn go too.

We carried Chiara/Amelia out, with the sisters behind us, and Andre locked the door. Only Pat McEvoy was in there now.

'Right,' he said. 'Harry and Samantha, you drop down first. Harry, you stand on the bins and I'll lower Amelia to you, then you lower her to Sammy. Clear?'

'Crystal.'

We barely made a sound until Andre smashed the glass out of the window with his boot. Then Declan came charging down the corridor like a startled boar. As he passed Maria and Isabella, he reached for his gun.

That was a mistake.

Maria suck out her left foot and he went flying straight into my boot. Night, night, sleep tight.

***

We didn't have to jump out the window. Shayna McBain was already there with a ladder.

'How the fuck…' I spluttered as I descended carrying Amelia over my shoulder in a fireman's lift.

'Not now, move quickly.'

Shayna led through the delivery gate where an old battered van was parked. It had SAM Same Day Delivery emblazoned on its sides, but when she opened the back doors, it seemed to be a converted ambulance. There was a bed, a stretcher, oxygen, an ECG, bag valve masks, a defibrillator…

Now it was Andre's turn to curse. 'What the holy fuck?' he gasped.

'Trust me. It's for your own safety, there's a lot of bad shit going down out here in jungle land tonight.'

We laid Amelia on the bed and strapped her in. There were four of us in the back. Shayna and Sammy were still on the street.

'You coming?'

'No, we've gotta be somewhere else. Micky Wall will drive you straight to the Langone. I'll call ahead. Tell them to prepare for emergency surgery.,'

'Eh? The Presbyterian is closer...' said Andre.

'Micky Wall?' I said.

'And how do you know Sammy?'

'Later! No time.'

Shayna slammed the back doors shut and thumped them three times with her fist. The driver – the unknown quantity Micky Wall – slammed the ambulance into first and put his foot down.

***

The woman born Chiara but currently known as Amelia listened intently. The Ox had left. That was the first piece of good news. The second was, although he'd thrown her back on the mattress, he had neglected to chain her back up. All she had to do was... someone was at the door. Linden! It had to be Johnny Linden. And it was. Except now he was holding a Glock and didn't look so friendly.

'You shouldn't have done that Amelia. I was being nice to you.'

'I know, I'm sorry. I was desperate. Please let me go, Johnny. You know this is wrong.'

'What I know is I can't trust you. Come on, get up. We're leaving this dump.'

As she stood up, he hesitated. There was a noise outside. Footsteps. Talking. Two men, maybe three. Linden stepped back into the shell of the restaurant.

Chiara listened intently but couldn't make out what was being said. She opened the door.

There were two men. Unknown to her. Both Italian-looking. The first man, heavyset and in his early thirties, was holding a Browning Buck Mark.

'C'mon, Mick, we're friends here. Lower the piece.'

'You first,' Johnny Linden replied. He had his back to the door to the old service area but clearly wanted to be somewhere else.

She was about to intervene when the heavyset man said, 'That ain't how this works.'

Then the second man spoke. 'Hey, Amelia, you's wanted.'

The accent was straight out of Newark.

'She's staying here, barked Linden unconvincingly.

The heavyset man let loose his full magazine.

Johnny Linden did the dance of death up against the door. But something hit her at the top of her chest, an inch or two above her heart.

The force of it sent her crashing into the wall. She was out cold when she hit the floor.

***

If the bloke who taught Micky Wall to drive hadn't had a coronary by lesson three, he deserved some sort of medal. Wall tapped the gas a few times then buried the pedal into the floor. Red lights, traffic lanes and speed limits meant nothing to the guy. As Randy Rhoads's guitar solo on Crazy Train soared, he must have hit seventy steaming through built-up areas where the average speed limit was 30. Yet no cops stopped us. How could they? Even if they hadn't been tied up at the siege, they could never have kept up. It was terrifying. Even hard-boiled Maria reached over and gripped my hand tightly waiting for the crash that didn't come.

'What is this?' she asked Andre. 'Why is an ambulance disguised as a courier van?'

'I can only assume there are people out there who we have to avoid at all costs, presumably people who want to kill us. Or at least some of us.'

'But who has the facilities to provide a vehicle like this?' I pondered, holding tight to the edge of the bed as Wall made a sharp right.

'Little agencies with three letter names,' he suggested. 'If we're talking RICO, the resources for bringing down criminal gangs and racketeers are massive.'

'Understood. But how is Shayna McBain involved?'

Andre said nothing. But now I knew for certain that he knew.

Maybe ten miles later, and in well under nine minutes, Micky Wall skidded to an abrupt halt outside the emergency room entrance with a mighty *Kerrang!* of a screech.

There were paramedics there already waiting with a trolley, along with uniformed cops. Wall appeared by my side, looking as nonchalant as a sunbather on a St Tropez beach.

'Where the fuck did you learn to drive like that?' I asked as I pumped his hand.

'Mosul,' he said.

'Green Berets?'

'Gotta go,' he said bluntly. 'Miss McBain might need me. Ciao.'

I gave him a thumbs up and looked over to the hospital entrance. Amelia was being wheeled in with her mother and aunt close behind. Two of the cops remained outside. I should have realised – I had noticed the difference between her and her cousin's eyes immediately and dismissed it.

All this time I thought I was talking to Amelia it had actually been Chiara. I must be losing my grip.

Andre walked over, puffing on a Marlboro Red.

'Since when have you smoked?'

'Since Mr Wall's Wild Ride. Jeez, I thought we were goners.'

I nodded. I started speaking my thoughts out loud. 'It makes sense coming here. They know Amelia is hurt and presumably want to hurt her more, so therefore they will have people watching local hospitals.'

'Yep, they wouldn't think we'd be dropping her off over here on 1st Avenue.'

'Meet you back here, mate. first thing,' I said. 'Hopefully she'll be able to talk to us then.'

'Okay, 8am?'

'Cool. Man, stealth ambulances, a special forces driver, armed cops…your Shayna is something else.'

His brow furrowed, like he wanted to say something. Instead he muttered, 'She's full of mysteries, and that's for sure…'

'A riddle wrapped in a mystery inside a Fred Perry.'

Andre grinned. 'Wasn't it Albert Einstein who said, the most beautiful thing we can experience is the mysterious.'

'You and you're fucking quotes. All I'd say is it's a shame old Albie ain't with us now to help decipher all this. Shayna may be beautiful but this mess ain't.'

'The thing is our work ain't finished, H. If McEvoy was telling the truth and they're going to make a move on Johnny tonight, then…'

'Then we need to get to Chiara before it comes on top. You know this Santa Monica Steakhouse joint.'

'Yeah. It was shut down months ago.'

'If it's where she is, might that be where Shayna was heading?'

'Makes sense. We could get there in twenty minutes.'

'Or we could let Buster know and let the NYPD steam in.'

He tapped his pockets.

'Our phones are back at the restaurant. There's a pay phone just over there.'

'Yeah. Got any change?'

***

It was unlucky for the two Jersey boys that Shayna and Sammy had followed them into the steakhouse and had the drop on them long enough for Sammy to scoop Amelia-Chiara off the floor. And unlucky for the two women that three more of the bastards were waiting outside to knock them out and load all three of the women into the trunk of their GMC Yukon XL.

They also took John Linden's corpse, inside a body bag, which was weighted and tossed into the Hudson.

***

I saw Buster arrive, with three uniformed cops, as our cab pulled up outside.

'Stand back until we secure the premises,' he barked.

I shrugged. He was in and out within five minutes.

'Anyone there?'

'Not a soul. But there is blood splattered about and signs of a scuffle.'

'Can we...' asked Andre, moving towards the door.

'No, you cannot go trampling over my crime scene. Forensics are on their way. There's nobody in there, but somebody was kept in the cold room, who we'll presume it was Amelia until it's proved otherwise.'

I nodded. He didn't know it was more likely to have been Chiara. He'd find out soon enough.

'Someone lost a lot of blood though. We'll check the dabs.'

'In the meantime, we need to talk to you about a coup that's happening tonight.' I said.

I explained quickly, with Andre throwing in extra detail.

Buster went quiet and walked out of earshot for a conversation. He returned with wearing an expression half of frustration and half of determination.

'This it's how it's going to be. The NYPD is going to protect G... Infantino.' He squeezed those words out with extreme reluctance. 'He will basically be under house arrest. But nobody, not Jersey, not Boston and not Guiliano Clarini will be able to get close to him and we'll take down anyone who tries.'

Behind him two of the cops were putting crime scene tape across the door.

I tried to have a conversation. 'I guess you have some kind of entente cordiale with Johnny Baby.'

'I'm afraid I don't speak French,' The Prince said gruffly.

Andre translated. 'You've got an understanding. Not a deal but a situation where he keeps things on an even keel.'

'If that changes and a maniac like Guilio takes over, all those old certainties are flushed down the gurgler,' I added.

'That's about the size of it,' Buster said grimly.

***

The cops departed in a hurry.

Andre sighed. 'So what you gonna do, bud? Head back to the hotel and party with Mr Jim Beam and Miss Ice-cold Rocks?'

'My late night consultants! I did think about it, but no mate. While they're off protecting one bad guy from a worse guy, nobody is looking for Chiara.'

'I don't even know where we could start looking.'

'That's why we've got to nose around in there before CSI get here.'

'That's risky mate.'

'Not if we're quick...'

The smell hit us immediately.

'Jesus the stench, what is that?' howled Andre.

'I'd say a mix of sweat, piss and shit.'

'It reeks, man.'

I sniffed deeply. 'Yep, it smells like we've been stuck in a lift with Godzilla for a week, and he's been on an all-fibre diet. But come on we're not here for long.'

Buster and the cops have been looking for people. I was looking for something else and it didn't take long to find it. Past a door splattered like a Jackson Pollock, only in blood rather than paint, I saw a room with a haphazard half-chopped line of cocaine on the table, along with a credit card. Something had disturbed them. On the floor, by the table leg was a wallet which contained a couple more grams of Charlie, two condoms and a number of business cards, including one for a restaurant/nightclub I'd never heard of called Raven Nights. In the corner, against the wall, was a plastic bag containing a revolver, bullets, two standard issue military M67 hand grenades, and a wad of leaflets for the exact same nightclub.

'Do you know this place?' I said thrusting a leaflet under his nose.

'Yeah, it's Guilio's restaurant/club, his main legit business. The name's dumb, a play on the Ravenite Social Club in Little Italy where Gotti used to hang out.'

'Tell me something. If you were leaving this place in a hurry, with a hostage, and you were working for Guilio and at least one of you was probably injured, and you needed to get to a safe house, would it make sense to head here?'

'Yeah. I mean, there are other places, but the Raven is bigger and safer. I can't think of anywhere else I'd go, if I had to steer clear of Johnny Baby's businesses.'

'Then we'd better get there pronto.'

'Yeah, but whatever you do, don't call Tommy.'

'Where is Micky Wall when we need him?'

'Tucked up in bed if he's got any sense.'

'With Shayna?'

Jealousy flashed across Andre's face but he shrugged and said, 'Why not? Some guys have all the luck.'

The street outside of Raven Nights was full of luxury vehicles – Mercedes, BMWs, a Jag convertible, a couple of black SUVs and an incongruous pink Chevelle; almost of them had New Jersey or Boston plates.

'Looks like the gang's all here,' I said flatly.

We walked down the side of the restaurant to the back. The door to the kitchen was unguarded.

'Okay, I've got a plan.'

I picked up a brick and passed Andre one of the two grenades.

'How fast can you run?'

'I'm not Usain Bolt, but I've had my moments.'

'In 30 seconds' time, I want you to chuck this brick through the front window of this restaurant, and then put a live grenade under the nearest car and fuck right off. Get clear of the scene, then find a phone and tell Buster Campbell we have a situation here. Can you do that?'

'Throw, blow and go. I think so.'

'Good, it will create enough confusion for me to get through the kitchen and start looking for Chiara.'

'And if she's not here?'

'Then I'm completely fucked and it's been nice knowing you.'

We shook hands.

'Laters, mate,' I said.

'Yeah, laters. But Harry, make your own way back from here. Remember, no Tommy.'

I nodded. No Tommy for sure. I'd read him wrong all right.

'No Micky Wall either. I like my heart in my chest, not in my mouth.' Although someone like Wall would come in handy. If this worked, we'd need a get-away driver who could take off like Sebastian Vettel.

Johnny Baby answered the phone curtly, but his tone rapidly changed to a more respectful tone.

The caller sounded older than he was, and slower. He had a three-packs-a-day voice, with a wheezy layer of grit.

'We're all together,' he rasped. 'We keep hearing the name Clarini. This guy. His name is everywhere. He's too loud, too noticeable. He's annoying people who shouldn't be annoyed. He is your brother-in-law Giovanni, but can you vouch for him?'

Johnny sighed. He didn't need much thinking time. 'I cannot. He has become an embarrassment.'

The older man responded with an Italian proverb. 'La madre dei cretini é sempre incinta' – the mother of idiots is always pregnant.

'Si. He was controllable at the start, an obedient attack dog. But too much cocaine has eaten away what little brain he had. I was planning to deal with him...'

'Don't,' the voice said firmly. 'Lascia fare a noi.'

'Si padrino.'

***

When the brick flew through the front window followed seconds later by an exploding Lamborghini, both Guiliano Clarini and Shayna McBain had the same thought – Johnny Baby had rumbled the plot.

Guilio, who was sweating, fizzy-eyed and paranoid from excess cocaine, started gabbling excitedly, ordering his men to take defensive positions. It was at least eight minutes before he sent out a scout. The guy came back three minutes later looking bemused.

'There's no one out there except a black and white checking out the remains of Mikey's jalopey,' he said.

***

As soon as I heard the car blew up, I came in quietly through the back door. The kitchen staff were distracted by the commotion and so I managed to knock out two of them with an aluminium Ballerini wok before the third one saw my face.

He'd be out for a few hours too.

I made my way up the steel stairs to the first floor, taking them two at a time as the cries and shouts from the restaurant rose to a crescendo.

There was one overweight guard posted outside the second room on the left. I approached from his blindside quietly.

'Hey' I said softly. He nearly jumped out of his skin. The wok helped him sleep.

I helped myself to his brand new Smith & Wesson 686 and tried the door. It was locked, but not particularly heavy. I kicked it open with one solid boot. Bingo. Chiara was there, in a state, along with Shayna Ross and Sammy who were both bound and gagged. I released Shayna and gave her the spare revolver and whispered 'Back soon' to Sammy.

I peered out of the door. The corridor was clear, so I tried my luck with the door opposite. Shayna followed me through. As I'd hoped, it was an office overlooking the main road. I approached the window and looked over gingerly. The only person out there was a lone cop walking away from the club and towards his car. I figured they must have convinced him the explosion had nothing to do with them.

I needed to convince him otherwise. I took out the second grenade and thought for a moment.

Shayna opened the window. 'Do it,' she said.

I threw the grenade at a parked car over the road. The blast almost knocked the cop of his feet. He was straight onto his radio calling for back-up.

Job done. I went back across the corridor, Shayna untied Sammy while I checked on Chiara. She was unconscious but breathing. The question was, should I risk taking them back out through the kitchen. It was either that or barricade ourselves into yet another room. Fight or flight?

I expected most of the mob to be outside the front with weapons drawn.

'C'mon, let's go,' I said. I gave Samantha my gun.

'I'll carry Chiara. Shayna can lead us down the stairs, Sammy, you're the rear guard. When we get through the kitchen, throw a right and walk through the carpark.'

I said a silent prayer that the lot would have another exit. The odds had to be good, right? A big carpark, a busy restaurant. To have one exit and entrance would be nuts.

***

At his table downstairs, Guilio Clarini did what he always did in a moment of stress. He chopped half a gramme of cocaine into four fat lines and demolished them.

***

Chiara came to on the way down. Her hand went straight to the bandaged wound above her heart.

'She needs a doctor,' said Shayna.

When we reached the kitchen, the staff were still where I left them. Out cold.

'Shayna, barricade the door to the restaurant please. If nothing else it'll delay them.'

I heard a thud behind me and swivelled. Samantha had gone down. One of the kitchen staff, a small burly guy with eyebrows so untrimmed they looked like beetles, had come round and had got hold of Sammy's gun. Shayna turned around, her Glock in hand.

'Drop it!' he barked. 'Drop it or the broad gets it.'

He turned to me. He was one-eyed, short but burly with a prison tattoo on his right wrist. He smelt of spliffs and caked-on sweat.

'You. Put the woman on the floor,' he barked.

I nodded and complied, tucking Chiara into a corner. She was unconscious again anyway. The floor was probably the best place for her.

'Now put your hands up and turn around away from me.'

Again, I did what he asked. Even though I knew what was coming next. Ahead of me I could see a saucepan full of pasta boiling. Out of reach for now, but if I could get to it... *WHAM!*

The little bastard had punched me in the back of my head which stung a bit. As I staggered forward, getting closer to the boiling saucepan, he levelled his handgun at Shayna.

'Unblock that fucking door and open it, or I'll blow the heads off of both of your friends.'

Rubbing the back of my head and moving backwards slowly, I looked down at Chiara. Her eyes were open.

'She'll do it,' I muttered, nodding towards Shayna. 'Come on Shay, we need to get out of here alive.'

The little chef sneered. I could tell he was thinking 'no way' even as Chiara rose slowly behind his back and kicked the gun out of his hand, following through with a karate double punch.

When he didn't drop immediately, she finished him off with a vicious chop to his throat that must have shattered his windpipe. Shit. The woman was lethal.

'Shame he wasn't as tough as his steaks,' she said.

'A bit harsh,' I said, retrieving her gun from the floor.

'Not at all. The perv helped beat up Shayna when we got here and he was creeping around Sammy when he brought food up, rubbing his little shrivelled cock up against her. I'd say he had it coming.'

Maybe he deserved that pasta water shower after all.

I could see the thought flash through Shayna's mind as she glanced over at it twice while she put the last touches to her barricaded door. Morality trumped revenge in the end.

'Come on, time to go,' she said.

Chiara looked a bit wobbly. I grabbed her. 'Hey, don't tire yourself, lean on me. I'll help you out.'

She draped her arm around my neck and we walked.

'That was a great combo, kid.'

'I've had lessons since I was little. So had Amelia. It's one of the odd parallels in our lives. Without knowing each other, we both became karate black belts.'

'Good on you. Let's get you out of here.'

Behind me, Shayna helped Sammy to her feet and pocketed a couple of kitchen knives. You never know when they could come in useful. Then together we plodded towards the exit, slowly but determined. Like pensioners getting the best seats at bingo.

***

In the alley behind the restaurant, Kevin Malone watched the Cockney dick and the three bitches leave through the kitchen door. He could hear his people trying to smash their way into the kitchen but for now he was on his own. Malone had been hurt in the explosion. Blood was trickling down his neck. But he wasn't going to let these scumbags get away with it.

'Hey,' he called, raising a lethal .357 Magnum. 'Stand still and listen good. This is how it ends for you, pricks. I'm going to shoot Tyler first, then I'm gonna rape this high society bitch until her cunt bleeds. And when I'm done with her, I'll do the same with you two.'

He moved in closer to Shayna on the 'you' and gave her an open-handed slap. A big mistake. She lashed out with a kitchen knife, slashing him with across his left cheek.

'Motherfucker!' He roared at her and pointed the Magnum.

A shot was fired, but not by Malone. The shot came from the carpark. Malone hit the floor, barely conscious. Shayna stepped forward and embedded the smaller of the kitchen knives between his ribs. He gave a low gasp of pain. Then she produced the larger one and slashed him across the groin. Malone screamed like an Inishmore banshee.

'Say goodbye to your little friend,' she sneered.

I scanned the carpark apprehensively. The mystery shooter emerged from the shadows. It was Micky Wall.

'Micky! How the fuck did you find us?'

Wall smiled and glanced at Shayna.

'Hey sis, doesn't he know about the trackers?'

'There's a lot he don't know,' she laughed.

***

As the black Chrysler executive drove past the Raven nightclub, Tommy Bryne heard his passenger gasp. The man in the back could see Giulio's guys, made-men from Jersey and the remnants of the Boston Irish mob, being handcuffed and thrown roughly into the back of meat wagons. He couldn't see Giulio but the gig was up.

'Drive on,' Sir Timothy told Tommy. 'Get me to JFK. I'll get the first available flight.'

'What about your bags, sir?'

'They're at the Hyatt. Have them shipped over. None of that is important. I've got my passport, my wallet.'

'And the girl?'

Storey thought for a moment. She was a cutie. Mexican with big brown eyes, 13-years-old. Just how he liked them.

'Send her back to the agent. He'll be paid in full.'

He sat calculating for a moment. 'Tommy, listen, nobody must know I was ever here. This trip never happened. You never picked me up, I never booked a room at the hotel, I had no guests.'

'Understood.'

'Good man.'

Sir Timothy sat back and counted out a $200 tip he would put into Tommy's breast pocket when he got out. Loyalty had its own rewards.

***

Micky Wall made good time to the Langone and while Shayna spoke to the medical staff, Andre rang Buster to let him know to call the dogs off. Both cousins were safe, Giulio was either collared or dead, Tim was on the missing list, Johnny Baby was back in charge, and the threat of a mob coup was over.

***

Moments after Micky Wall had driven them out of the carpark, and from the chaos, Giulio Clarini had limped through the backdoor of the kitchen and headed for the carpark. He'd been shot in the left arm and it hurt like fuck. Luckily he was right-handed.

Sucking on his Cohiba cigar, Giulio placed his Glock on top of the Mercedes as he fumbled for his keys. He didn't hear the three men walk up behind him and only felt the first two of the bullets.

One of the men turned over his body, another stripped him of his wallet, his jewellery – including a Rolex Oyster and a hefty diamond encrusted gold bracelet – and the wraps of cocaine that were in his pockets, the third picked up Giulio's cigar and stubbed it out on forehead.

When they were done, the men returned to their black and white, turned on the siren, and drove away at high speed.

Chapter 11

Day 6
Saturday.
6.55am John F. Kennedy International Airport.

The 8.05am British Airways flight from JFK to Heathrow would get in at 8pm, UK time. The ticket had cost Sir Timothy Storey $400 – which was nothing, and which would be worth a fortune if it meant getting out of New York without being noticed.

His watch said 6.55. About 15minutes before boarding time. He yawned and bought a coffee and a copy of the New York Times and then sat quietly in a remote corner, flicking through it. The nightclub fiasco had made the late edition, reported as a suspected gang war. Two men had been murdered. One of them was Giuliani Clarini.

Jesus. That was it. Game over.

At least Johnny wouldn't suspect his involvement. Business was safe.

An American voice over the speaker system announced that flight BA 178 to London Heathrow was boarding. He would get through quickly and upgrade onboard. Tuck himself in a window seat and get some kip. The last two days were had been an inconvenient waste of time.

The queue was still short, and he was at the boarding gate in minutes. The BA staff member smiled so sweetly as she checked his passport that Sir Tim didn't even notice her nod to the armed security officer a few feet behind her.

In fact he took no notice of him until the man grabbed his elbow and guided him off down a corridor for an unscheduled meeting with NYPD detective inspector Buster Campbell and two uniformed police officers. As one officer read him his Miranda Rights, Sir Tim felt like his life-force was slowly ebbing out of his body.

He exercised his right to remain silent but inside he was screaming. Harry fucking Tyler. The fucking indignity. Him, a Mensa-level mastermind outsmarted by a piss-pot Essex boy private eye.

***

8.05am

Both patients were sitting up in bed when we sauntered in. Even patched up with drips in their arm, the girls looked a lot healthier than Maria and Isabella who had plainly not slept a wink. Make that mother and auntie – the story we needed to get to the bottom of.

Maria got up and kissed me on the cheek. 'We're going to get coffee' – pronounced *coi-fee* – 'want anything?'

'Two cups of regular rocket fuel would be perfect,' said Andre.

'You well enough to chat?' I asked the real Amelia.

'I am, Mr Tyler. And thank you for all your help.'

'Yes thanks, Harry,' Chiara said weakly.

'So you and your lookalike cousin, any chance you could fill us in?'

'Chiara found me on Facebook yonks ago. We've been friends on there since 2006. I couldn't believe it when I first saw her photograph. We're practically identical, as you know.'

She smiled.

'Tell me about it!'

'We talked and talked online and then on the phone and gradually the pieces fell into place. Her mother, auntie Isabella, had told her that her real father wasn't Giulio but an Englishman, an accountant who cooked the family books, an Englishman by the name of Timothy. You're ahead of me, I'm sure.'

'Sir Timothy Storey,' said Andre.

'Exactly. Now, I knew I was adopted and that my parents weren't my birth parents – or so I thought. It's slightly more complicated than that. Turns out, and this is confirmed by DNA, that we both had the same father, and our mothers were identical twin sisters. But my poor old mum back home never knew she was raising her husband's love child.

'So there it is. I am the daughter of Sir Timothy Storey and Maria Infantino; Chiara is the daughter of Sir Timothy Storey and Isabella Clarini. Only Guilio has no idea he's been firing blanks all these years.'

'The word is had,' said Andre. 'I'm afraid Chiara's mobster dad was found dead in his restaurant carpark at 2am this morning.'

'Break it to them gently, why don't you?' I snapped.

'It's okay Harry, there's no love lost there,' Chiara said.

I nodded and held up my hand to stop the conversation for a moment to process the information.

'So let me get this straight. Posh boy Tim was having transatlantic flings with two women who were both married to the mob?'

'The fat fuck has got a death wish,' Andre said flatly.

Amelia interjected. 'My father has indeed been having a fling as you say with my mother, Maria for decades. Very discretely. In London and New York and at least once in Positano. But Chiara was the result of a one-night stand between my father and aunt Isabella.'

'Right…'

'Auntie Issy was dating Guilio at the time but was still virgo intacta. So let's just say she moved their relationship on very quickly, letting him think she couldn't resist him any longer. So he thinks Chiara is his and thinks we look alike because our mothers are twins.'

'That would make sense,' said Andre.

'Johnny doesn't know that my mother had me because as soon as she realised she was up the duff, she went into a convent for six months.'

'Do Catholic men like that?'

'Of course, six months as a novice, it's the ultimate proof of innocence. He didn't even know I existed.'

'And what would Guilio have done if he found out Chiara wasn't his?'

'He'd have killed Daddy. Shot him dead. No question. It's an honour thing. That's part of the reason my father brought in the Irish mob – as insurance. If Guilio found out, because of us, the Malones would have got him out of Dodge.'

'And the fake robbery at Infantino's?'

'That was Daddy's idea. The primary purpose wasn't to steal but to weaken and belittle Johnny Baby, which of course Guilio loved.'

'If a boss can be robbed so easily, how can he be respected?' I said. Our suspicions were confirmed.

'Exactly. But when you cracked the case Mr Tyler, you made a very bad enemy in Guilio. He wanted you dead, just as much as Daddy probably still wants me dead before I can spill the beans and see his empire come toppling down.'

'And Chiara wants that too?'

'Of course.'

She looked over at her cousin, now dozing lightly. 'Bless her. The funny thing about Chiara and I, Mr Tyler, is that as soon as we first started talking, we realised we were so alike, the same sense of humour, the same taste in music, and in men.'

'She's likes them druggy too, does she?'

'She likes them rebellious too.'

'So wait when she was pretending to be you, she was sleeping with Tippy Jay?'

'We're like sisters, sisters share.'

Andre laughed. 'And Jay was too stoned to tell the difference.'

'Too stoned for anything most of the time.'

'Well, I hope the experience was as disappointing as I'd imagine it to be.'

'I'm sure it was,' she laughed.

Andre still looked puzzled. Sorry to sound like I'm one nugget short of a Happy Meal, but is this right? English aristocrat, Sir Tim, your dear daddy, was in league with a mafia headcase and had a plan to take over Infantino's patch with the backing of an ambitious New Jersey mob. And he cultivated the Boston mob as insurance against Guilio, his partner in treachery.'

'Pretty much. But don't forget Daddy had been handling the accounts for all of their legitimate businesses. He had their trust, and he knew their secrets.'

'So the puppet master emerges.'

'But that wasn't enough to keep him safe, because of what Chiara and I found out.'

We both looked blank.

'It's all on the USB stick I gave you, Mr Tyler. There's a lot of information about the businesses and the accounting, a huge spider's web of offshore holding corporations and the shell companies; but beyond that, there's plenty about how my oh so respectable libidinous love rat of a father's very dirty secrets – secrets that we have managed to uncover over the years, with a little help from Sammy, who you've both met.'

'And what's she to Shayna McBain?' asked Andre.

'I don't know a Shayna McBain.'

'This is a lot to take in,' I said. 'Your father seeks to do you harm because you know his business secrets?'

'It's a lot more than that, Mr Tyler. We accessed he and Guilio's emails and WhatsApp messages. What you'll find on that USB stick are the details of their business connections, their underhand links to other crime gangs – in Daddy's case the Boston Irish, in Guilio's the New Jersey mafia – and also their Masterplan, which is or was to move against Johnny Infantino, to weaken and then eliminate him in order to take over his territory and run it as part of a wider crime gang run by Uncle Guilio with my father pulling the strings. They want to run the whole eastern seaboard.'

'How did you access all this in the first place?' asked Andre.

'Let's just say he wasn't very smart with password security. I found all of his passwords on the first page of the little black book he keeps in his office draw. I would have guessed it anyway, ScottL76 – he went to a school called Scott Lidgett and seems inordinately proud of it. He even has a school picture on his office wall, from his first year. 1976.'

I nodded but this threw me. Scott Lidgett was a comprehensive school in Bermondsey, as rough as you like. How did that equate with Sir Timothy, the genteel posho?

Amelia was still talking. 'Oh yes, on the USB stick you will also find some of the rather unpleasant child pornography that they were both partial too.'

'Child porn?'

That was unexpected.

'The worst. And there's worse. Underage girls. Daddy is evil, Mr Tyler. He raped me when I was nine and he didn't stop until I was old enough and strong enough to fight back. He…'

Maria and Isabella returned with coffees on a tray and Amelia clammed up.

'Shall we stop?'

'No please, ask away.'

'I think I understand all that. But what were you planning to do with all of that acquired info? Were you intending to blackmail your father?'

'No, we weren't doing it for money. We just wanted them to stop. To abandon their plan and in my father's case to retire, step away from the day to day running of his legitimate side of his business and hand the reins to my mother, who was blissfully unaware of any of this until very recently.'

Andre stroked his chin. 'So you and Chiara switched identities to throw them off the scent?'

'No. We swapped identities because we could. For a game, Mr Schweitzer. For a laugh. We used to mimic each other's accents all the time. We did it one time with Jason and it was child's play to fool him, and so we thought why not take a holiday in each other's lives? It just so happened that our 'vacation' coincided with the endgame of their takeover plan.'

'So why come to New York in the first place?'

'I'd met Jason in London, at a Conflict gig in New Cross. He was quite tough and a little less druggy back then, he was switched on politically and he was heading home to the Village. So it made sense. I wanted to be near Chiara and my real family and get away from the stifling orthodoxy of the Virginia Water Storeys. And of course, to execute our Masterplan. That's why Daddy hired Mr Tyler to find me before I could "blow the bloody doors off" his little empire. You thought you were hunting for me to save me, you were actually a scout for the hunters.'

'Shit... I...'

Maria interrupted. 'Maybe you should give her a rest now, Harry. She's been through a lot. We all have.'

'Of course.' I gave Amelia a peck on the cheek.

'Look into Daddy's background,' she said softly. 'I know you have the means. You'll be amazed. It seems Sir Timothy Storey was never quite what he seems either.'

***

Ten minutes later we were outside of the hospital.

'The abuse, the child porn, the child sex... if that was all on the USB stick, why didn't Shayna tell us?'

'I dunno,' Andre answered unconvincingly.

'You do know, mate. You know something.'

'Okay. Because I trust you, but don't let on for fuck's sake. She works for the District Attorney, her background is in the military police. But she's been seconded to the FBI for this job.'

I said nothing. 'They sent her in to me for two reasons. Firstly because I was doing work with Infantino, I had that connection; secondly because I could find out which cops were on the take quicker than Buster Campbell could.'

'And you never thought to warn me?'

'Mate, they didn't want anyone knowing. It was need-to-know only. It was easier for them to work through me than it was to try to get info from mob connected insiders. I caught her out a couple of weeks in, she swore me to secrecy and of course I've been co-operating not least because she made it quite clear they would close down my business if I didn't. But in fairness H, she's very handy. Not just because of her connections, but also because she's a master hacker.'

Well finally, the truth. Good. For a moment I thought I'd lost a mate to the dark side.

'How about the Mod thing? A cover?'

'No that's genuine. Even federal agents need a bit of rest and recreation time.'

I smiled. 'So, breakfast?'

'Sounds good. I know a place.'

He led the way down the street to a homely cafe.

'So what plans have you got for your last day, Harry?'

'My plans are very liquid, mate. A few beers, then hit the vodka.'

'Well how about we take in that Agnostic Front show tonight? It'll be an eye opener.'

'And an ear-batterer. Yeah. Why not?'

'We should catch up with Buster first. Make sure he's happy.'

'Sure. But let's eat first.'

Breakfast was spectacular. A mountain of pancakes, soaked in syrup, with the funny old Yank bacon and sausages.

Over my third cup of coffee, the idea of coming back to the States kicked in.

'If you could go anywhere in the States, where would you recommend? Away from the cities, I mean.'

Andre thought for a moment.

'I'd go south along the Blue Ridge Mountains and head east from Vegas into the deserts of Utah and Colorado,' he said finally. 'But rural Maine is just as good, and you have to see the sun setting in the Pacific off Malibu before you die… Mate, you could spend your whole life driving here and never see it all.'

'I can imagine. But I've not got a lifetime. I've got a day and a bit.'

'One more day and I'd have said get to Newark, fly up to Harpswell and treat yourself to a Maine lobster wrap. It's worth it. I mean you could do that today and swerve Agnostic Front.'

'After the build up you gave them? No. I've got to see them for myself. I will be back, mate. And I will take your advice.'

'Okay, and if I were ever to get back over to the UK and Ireland, where would you recommend for me? Obviously I've sampled the delights of Silvertown and Peckham as you know.'

'In Ireland, the ring of Kerry. It's stunning. And on mainland, the Lakes or the English Peak District at the end of the Pennines. The best motoring road is the Cairnwell Pass, up in Jockland near Pitlochry. It's the highest main road in the whole of the UK. It used to be the link road between the highlands and the lowlands. It runs by the Spital of Glen Shee, and what they call the Devil's Elbow, through open moorland. You follow the

River Shee, there's a steep climb up to the elbow, and the views of the glen are mind-blowing.'

'Why is it called the Devil's Elbow?'

'It's a double hairpin bend. Imagine taking that on with Micky Wall driving…'

***

Chapter 12

Eleven hours later
Awesome. Shocking. Aggressive. Louder than war. Just some of the words that sprung to mind when Agnostic Front finished their set at Otto's Shrunken Head. Their music was 'New York Hardcore', which meant it had emerged from a mixed marriage of working-class punk and heavy metal with the same spirit of togetherness that bands like the Cockney Rejects and The Business had channelled.

There were even crossed hammers scrawled on the graffiti-blitzed bog walls but as Andre explained, here it meant working-class unity, not West Ham United.

Everybody in the room was soaked to the skin with sweat. At one point I found myself in the middle of a circle pit with Shayna McBain, looking hotter than lava in a studded denim waistcoat, with a bullet belt, tight ripped black trousers, and a matching t-shirt.

One minute we were pogoing, trying to avoid the lunging crowd, the next we were kissing deep and long as Roger Miret led the crowd through, *'From the East Coast to the West Coast, gotta, gotta, gotta go/Two sides of a revolution, gotta, gotta, gotta, go...'*

We didn't stop tongue-wrestling until the song ended.

After I lost her in the melee, so I waited at the bar with Andre and Sammy who updated me on the titles of mosh heavy songs like Rage and Today, Tomorrow Forever.

'What did you think?' asked Sammy.

'Awesome. That combo, the roaring guitar and vocals, distorted and angry, the loud driving bass riffs, the insistent drums... awesome is the only word. They seemed to suck every ounce of oxygen and scepticism out of the room.'

'Nicely put,' she said.

'Yeah, you should try writing for a living man.'

'It might be safer. Hey, anyone see where Shayna went?'

'She went home to get changed and freshen up. Said she might see us later,' said Sammy.

'Where's later?'

'I thought we could go on to a late bar, like The Four-Faced Liar which stays open until 4am. It's about three miles from the Plaza.'

'Cool. I don't have to check out until 11am. Then I guess I'll get a taxi to JFK as I can't imagine Mr Byrne will be on call now. Or that my free limo service still exists.'

Andre signed. 'Shame he was a wrong'un, you liked him didn't you?'

'Yeah. He was just doing his job, I guess.'

'That's what the guards said at Auschwitz,' Andre grunted before departing for a gypsy's.

The security men had started clearing out the venue ahead of a later show, but they seemed happy enough to let us carry on drinking leisurely at the bar.

'There's another band coming on, which means a fresh audience.'

'Fresh and thirsty.'

'Odd they haven't moved us out,' said Sammy.

I nodded. 'Maybe they've taken pity on us old bastards, I'm not including you in that description.'

She smiled and her whole face lit up. A revelation. I suddenly noticed how hot Sammy was, especially punked up in leathers. Mascara and make-up had brought out the beauty in her handsome features just as surely as the night had brought out the twinkle in her eyes.

I bought three large Hennessey brandies and gave one to Sammy and one to Andre returned, already the worse for wear.

She looked bemused when he and I touched glasses and made a toast.

'Never above you...' I said.

'Never below you…' he replied, touching my glass.

'Always with you,' we said as one and downed half of our respective brandies.

Andre laughed, kissed Sammy on the cheek, and said, 'Wives and girlfriends…'

'May they never meet,' I replied.

'You guys,' said Samantha pulling a face.

'Come on, I'll flag us down a cab,' said Andre who seemed barely capable. Sammy led the way to the door but suddenly stopped abruptly. She had seen what we saw a moment later.

Our path was blocked by The Ox.

'You're the cunts who fucked things up,' he roared, his red face a seething mass of resentment.

He grabbed hold of Sammy, his huge hands squeezing her shoulders like an arcade claw machine and hurled her to the floor.

'Leave her the fuck alone,' I yelled.

I picked up a bar stool and wrapped it round his head. He didn't seem to notice. As we found out later, the Ox was on phencyclidine – Angel Dust to you and me. Take that and you feel stronger and bolder, and you don't feel pain. The shit also makes you delirious and psychotic and usually causes convulsions. So not quite Bruce Banner's gamma rays.

He came at me awkwardly like he was having trouble walking. I grabbed another stool and stood over Sammy, trying to shield her but he swung a fist the size of a bear's paw that knocked me off my feet and stung like buggery.

Now he turned to face Andre. Again, I noticed how stiff his legs were. Arthritis? Must be.

'Andre! Chips and peas! Chips and peas!' I yelled, hoping against hope that he wasn't too out of it to pick up on the meaning.

The Ox looked utterly baffled.

Andre got it. He kicked at the big man's left knee with his steel-capped boot. The Ox didn't register the pain, but he did topple forwards like a pole-axed bison. Later we found the kick had knocked his patella out of place.

The two watching security men didn't know what to do.

'Get the other knee,' I shouted, as I got up and helped Sammy to her feet to front them.

Andre duly obliged, leaving the crimson-faced heavyweight immobile. He started pointlessly dragging himself towards us.

I looked at the security men. 'You saw what happened. This meathead attacked this woman and then tried it on with us. How do you want to be?'

The men looked at The Ox as he pulled himself along, a picture of incoherent impotence, and stood aside for us.

Outside Andre gave me a brief but ecstatic hug.

'Now I finally I realise the point of that rhyming slang shit,' he said.

'You're such a great dental,' I said straight-faced.

'What? What's that one? I don't know it.'

'Later, mate. Later.'

***

We never made The Four-Faced Liar. Andre sobered up and went home. Me and Samantha carried on drinking at the Plaza, convincing ourselves it was the safest available course of action on the grounds that no more half-witted mobster thugs would show up there.

Nobody had thought to tell Shayna McBain, who turned up at the Liar an hour later, dolled up to the nines with a view to seducing the English detective who had tickled her fancy and would surely have fancied her tackle had he got to see what she was wearing under her leather coat.

Chapter 13

Day 7

Sunday. Midtown Manhattan.

'Wake up, sleepy head.'

A woman. Her hand shook me and I groaned slightly. What was this, déjà vu? Or déjà screw? She walked away, and I opened one eye. The clock said 7.02am. I could smell her perfume. It wasn't Tricia the airhostess. It was Samantha who by the sound of it was having a shower. I closed my eyes, and it all flooded back to me.

We'd come up to my room to watch TV and drain the mini-bar. One thing led to something entirely different. Very different. Sammy certainly liked to take control. She was so forceful in bed, pounding down on top of me, that I almost felt that I was the woman in the equation. Or maybe a stallion under the whip of a champion jockey like Richard Hughes.

Sammy had also mentioned having a torture room back at hers. For the next time I was over.

Oh god. That was twice I'd cheated in a week. What happened in New York would definitely stay in New York.

There was a knock on the door. 'Housekeeping,' the woman said. I pulled on my discarded boxers, stepped over Sammy's bra and pants and opened the door a couple of inches to politely ask the chambermaid to come back later.

The maid was there but the first thing I saw was the business end of a Glock 17 with a fitted silencer pointed straight at my kisser.

The owner of the Glock was clearly Italian-American. I'd seen him with Clarino at Johnny Baby's gaff. He pushed me backwards roughly into the room and then again onto the unmade bed.

'You've been a real pain in the ass, Tyler, but guess what? You're going to pay for what you did to Guilio.'

I closed my eyes and prepared for the inevitable.

Pfft. A shot was fired from a silencer. I wasn't hit. Guilio's man wasn't there – well he was, but he was dead, with Shayna McBain looking down at him.

'They always make speeches don't they?' she laughed.

There was something different about her. For starters, the attention-grabbing chorizo-red lipstick and the unexpected smile on her face, but that dissipated the moment she noticed Sammy's underwear on the floor.

'So you had a little company last night did you?'

There was tension in her voice, and Shayna's freckles seemed to flare up in tandem.

'Yeah, I...'

The toilet flushed. The tap ran. Moments later Samantha emerged wearing nothing but a bath towel.

'You couldn't help yourself, could you?' Shayna hissed. She turned and left, wiping off her lipstick as she went. At the door she turned back and said, 'Don't touch the body, my boys will be up here to deal with it. Twenty minutes tops.'

'What's eating her?' shrugged Sammy.

'Not me, that's for sure.'

The heavy bruising across her collarbone, from where The Ox had gripped her, looked deeper and darker in the daylight.

'Shall we order breakfast?'

'Let's get the works.'

I rang down and asked for everything supersized. Samantha was almost entirely dressed when I got off the phone. Which was a pity.

'How do you and Shayna know each other? It seems an unlikely match, a soup kitchen hippie and a detective investigator. Unless of course you know each other because you're an undercover agent too.'

'Bingo,' she said.

'So Shayna was investigating the mob, and you were checking out the anarchists.'

'Yes. We knew each other from the Military Police days. This time, she had the tough guys, and I had the loons.'

'I was U/C too. We should exchange cases next time I'm over.'

'So I will see you again, will I then, Harry?'

'See me? Oh yeah, I'm coming back to New York baby and I'm gonna marry you for a green card.'

'You romantic bastard. You never know I might say it yes.'

I walked over and kissed her. We were still going strong when room service turned up.

'I'll take it from here, thanks.' I said, blocking his way and shoving a $5 dollar bill into his top pocket before taking the tray off him. 'I'm packing so everything is a mess right now.'

I brought the tray in and set it on the desk. Sammy was in the bathroom again.

'You eating?'

'I thought we should work up an appetite first,' she said, walking out stark naked.

She held me down as she rode me, like she was a cowgirl breaking in a bronco, leaning forward to bite my neck and shoulders as I gripped her hips to quicken the pace. We both came quickly and loudly.

It was just a relief she didn't flip me over and brand me with a hot iron. 'Property of Samantha, FBI (drippy hippy department).'

'Next time, pegging,' she said firmly.

My smile seemed genuine, my eyes said fuck that.

***

Epilogue #1

There was no drama getting to JFK. The Plaza booked me a limo, just as classy as Tommy Byrne's. I'm pretty sure the stuck-up concierge was glad to see the back of me. I overpaid the driver in cash – I'd barely made a dent on Johnny Baby's $500 up until now.

I had a little bit of an issue at the airport bar when I'd ordered an $18 pint of lager and the jobsworth bartender insisted on seeing my passport. I told him the only place I could pass for under thirty was down a mineshaft, but he didn't crack a smile.

I'd felt text alerts on my mobile all the way through airport security, and as I sat with my overpriced pint, I scrolled through them. There was one from Shayna McBain saying simply 'Sorry. Next time?', one from Amelia Storey saying 'Thank you', and two from Maria alluding to unfinished business. Sammy had sent graphic descriptions of her BSM plans for my return, and finally Amanda had texted asking what time I was due to land. An embarrassment of dishes.

I replied to Amanda first, feeling guilty, then sent short friendly responses to the others. I was debating whether to shell out for a second pint when a text came through from a number I didn't recognise that said simply, 'Dear Harry, please accept sincere apologies from our whole family. My sister behaved appallingly, my father is retiring from his job and if you're ever back in town and in need of a meal, you're always welcome in our home. Slán abhaile, N xoxo.' N. Noreen!

So maybe my gut feelings about Tommy Byrne weren't so wrong after all.

I texted back, drank up and headed up to the book store where I picked up the latest copy of Mad magazine, with a Lego cover, to read on the plane.

I was happily filing onto the aircraft with the other sheep when to my surprise I spotted Tricia Butler reprising her role as one of the stewardesses in first class.

'Harry,' she smiled. 'So pleased to see you.'

She guided me to my seat and returned promptly with a pre-flight flute of champagne and a cold can of Amstel.

'Your pals are on here again too.'

'The West Ham lads? We can barely move for coincidences today.'

'I'll talk to you later,' she said with a wink.

As she left, my phone beeped one more time before I switched it off. It was another unknown number and it said simply, 'Harry. Thank you. Enjoy yourself, it's later than you think. BC.' That made me smile. Buster Campbell was quoting the real Prince Buster.

First Class wasn't crowded so I had no company. I studied the menu and the movies and was reading the weak Hunger Games spoof in Mad when the lights went down for the films. I was about to turn on my seat light when Tricia came back.

'Mr Tyler, the captain will see you now,' she said primly.

Puzzled I got up and followed her behind the curtain where she pushed me into one of the plush toilets and locked the door behind her.

'Have you ever joined the Mile High Club, Harry?' she asked coquettishly.

'I have not.'

'Well now is your chance.'

I smiled. We kissed as passionately as teenagers, then Tricia broke away.

'Prepare for take-off,' she whispered as she pulled up her skirt and wriggled out of her black, corded lace Yves St Laurent panties.

'There's two ways we can do this,' she said, handing me an unwrapped condom. 'You sitting down with me on top, or you standing up and holding me… if you're strong enough.'

I was strong enough. But neither of us took that long to reach our destination. Tricia came first, digging her nails into my arse cheeks like she was popping zits, and I followed hard on her heels. She wiped herself clean with a tissue, then gave me a long lingering kiss and left first. It was almost like she'd done this before.

I relocked the door, promised myself this was definitely the last time I'd ever cheat on Amanda, and waited ninety seconds before following her.

There was nobody waiting.

I was about to walk back through to my seat when I heard a man with a strong foreign accent shouting. The only words I recognised were "Allahu Akbar!"

Oh shit! Here we go again…

To be continued in MYSTIC MAGUIRE: Tall Tales & Short Stories by Garry Bushell, scheduled to be published by Caffeine Nights in October 2026.

Epilogue II

Sir Timothy Storey was charged with racketeering and money-laundering related to criminal activities throughout New York City. The trial was due to take place in federal court in the Southern District of New York. If found guilty he was looking at 5 to 20 years in Sing Sing. After his initial hearing, Storey was granted bail in the sum of $3million dollars by United States District Judge Kim Da-Eun. He subsequently fled the country using a false passport sourced by his contacts in Boston, returning via Dublin to Britain – where he faced up to fourteen years behind bars for similar charges. Passing through airport security undetected, Storey melted into southeast London's murky and insular criminal underworld.

The NYPD working with the Met Police uncovered what they described as 'a vast international money-go-round' with millions of pounds lodged in coded accounts in London, New York, Liechtenstein, Switzerland, Jersey, and the Isle of Man. Police acknowledged that this was probably the tip of a far larger ice berg.

After the story broke, a Sunday Times investigation into Sir Tim's background revealed that the seemingly respectable accountant – who had been educated at Eton from the age of sixteen and then the Department Of Economics at Oxford University – had actually been born and raised on Deptford's Evelyn Street council estate. His father, Alan 'Iron Al' Storey, was a successful bank robber associated with the notorious Baker brothers 'firm'. He had paid for his son's education and his elocution lessons out of the proceeds of crime. Storey's marriage to the heiress Lady Gabriella Fortesque had secured his place in high society.

Storey was stripped of his knighthood – an act known as 'degradation' – by the Cameron government. The Home Secretary announced that if found in Great Britain, Storey would also face charges involving child sex, trafficking, and child pornography.

He was never convicted.

In November 2016 a man named as Oliver Bradley was executed by a Russian hit-woman nicknamed the Red Assassin by the tabloid press. His body was found riddled with bullets in The Prince Of Wales pub in Kennington, southeast London. Not a single eyewitness in the packed bar was able to give an adequate description of his killer.

Forensic analysis of Bradley's DNA later revealed his true identity to be the disgraced Timothy Storey. His story would inspire two television documentaries and a gritty British film starring Terry Stone which painted him as a class warrior. The movie, called The Outsider, was financed by businessmen from south London, Boston and New York.

Next in Garry Bushell's The Face series, book six – Harry Tyler: Behind Bars – *due in October 2027.*

Glossary of Slang

Ag – trouble, short for aggravation.

Alans – knickers (rhyming slang, Alan Whickers, archaic).

Apples - £20 notes (rhyming slang; apple cores = scores).

April – tool (rhyming slang; April Fool = tool = weapon).

Arthur – hard man (rhyming slang Arthur Mullard = hard; archaic).

Aris – arse (rhyming slang; Aristotle = bottle, bottle and glass = arse; see Queen Mum)

Bag – £1,000 (rhyming slang, bang of sand = grand)

Banged up – imprisoned

Bang to rights – caught red-handed; guilty.

Barney – trouble or fight (rhyming slang, Barney Rubble).

Barry – a big woman (rhyming slang, Barry McGuigan = a big'un)

Battle-cruiser – pub (rhyming slang, boozer).

Bent – Crooked or stolen goods

Bent – gay (see iron)

Beer tokens – pounds sterling (see sov)

Betty – Table (rhyming slang, Betty Gable = table)

Billy – amphetamines (slang from the cartoon character, Billy Whizz)

Bird – time in prison (bird lime = time)

Blade-runner – someone transporting stolen goods.

Blag – to rob, originally a pay-roll or money delivery in a public place.

Blagger – a robber

Boat – face (boat race = face; see also Chevy Chase).

Bob Hope – cannabis (rhyming slang, dope, see also puff).

The boob – prison.

To boost – to hot-wire a car.

Boracic – skint (rhyming slang, boracic lint = skint).

Bottle out – to lose one's nerve (see brick it).

Boutros – cocaine (rhyming slang, Boutros Boutros-Ghali = Charlie)

Brahma – beautiful, or something good.

Brahms and Listz – drunk (rhyming slang, Brahms and Listz = pissed).

Brass – prostitute (see also Tom, dripper).

Brick it – to bottle out, to lose your nerve.

Britney Spears – ears (rhyming slang).

Brown bread – dead (rhyming slang).

A bullseye – £50

A bung – a bribe

Bushel – neck (rhyming slang, bushel and peck; see also Gregory)

Butchers – a look (Butcher's Hook, rhyming slang)

Canister – head (see Swede)

Carpet – three months imprisonment

Cash and Carry, commit – suicide (rhyming slang, hari-kari)

Charlie – cocaine, see also Chas, sherbet, marching powder, nose-bag, Gianluca, Ying, gear, King Lear, lemo, Dave's mate).

Chavvy – a child (Romany)

China – mate (rhyming slang, china plate).

Chips – knees (rhyming slang, chips and peas).

Chiv – a knife.

The Church – Customs & Excise (C of E)

Clean – innocent.

Clobber – clothes (see also schmutta)

Cobblers – rubbish (rhyming slang, cobblers' awls = balls)

A cockle – £10 (rhyming slang, cockle and hen = ten).

Collar felt – to be arrested, as in "He had his collar felt").

Cream-crackered – tired (rhyming slang, knackered).

The Currant – The *Sun* newspaper (rhyming slang, currant bun)

Dabs – finger prints.

Daisy – a safe-breaking tool.

Darby – belly (rhyming slang, Darby Kelly = belly; see also Darby Kell)

Dave's mate – cocaine, from Chas and Dave, as used in the phrase "Is Dave's mate about tonight?"

Dental flosser – tosser (rhyming slang).

Dipper – a pick pocket.

The dog – the telephone (rhyming slang, dog and bone).

Donald – fuck (rhyming slang Donald Duck = fuck, as in 'Fancy a quick Donald?'; see also Posh & Becks = sex)

Doris – a woman.

Dot – rotten (rhyming slang, Dot Cotton).

A drink – a bribe, ranging from a drink to a nice drink to a handsome drink.

Dripper – see brass.

Drumming – house-breaking.

Dustbins – children (dustbin lids = kids).

An earner – easy money.

Elephants – drunk (rhyming slang, elephants trunk = drunk; see also Brahms, from Brahms & Liszt = pissed; all archaic)

Eyetie – Italian

Feds – the police

Fence – a receiver of stolen goods

The Filth – the police (see also Old Bill, cossers, rozzers, Plod, Feds, bogeys).

Firm – a gang.

To fit-up – to give or plant false evidence.

Flowery – cell (rhyming slang, Flowery dell)

Four-be – a Jew (rhyming slang, 4 be 2)

In the frame – to be the prime suspect.

Frankie – cut-throat razor (rhyming slang, Frankie Fraser)

A friend of ours – one of us. A friend of mine, means he seems OK but hasn't been fully referenced.

Gaff – a house, see also drum and gaff of a gaff (a mansion)

The Game – prostitution, as in on the game

Gary – toilet or anus (rhyming slang, Gary Glitter = shitter)

George Young – tongue (rhyming slang).

Gianluca – cocaine (rhyming slang, Gianluca Vialli = Charlie).

Gillian = blow job (from a Gillian Taylforth court case; see also a large G&T)

To give a pull – to impart words of advice.

Goldfish, to slip her the goldfish – sex (see poger).

Gold watch – Scotch (rhyming slang).

Graft – work, or piece of villainy.

A grass – an informer.

Gregory – neck (rhyming slang, Gregory Peck, see Bushel).

Grumble – vagina (rhyming slang, grumble & grunt)

Gypsy's – a piss (rhyming slang, Gypsy's kiss; see also slash, lash and Jimmy, from Jimmy Riddle – piddle).

Half-chat – mixed race.

Half-inch – pinch (rhyming slang).

Hampton – penis (rhyming slang, Hampton wick = prick).

Hand Grenades – AIDS (rhyming slang).

Hank Marvin – starving (rhyming slang).

Harry – semen (rhyming slang, Harry Monk = spunk)

A Henry – an eighth of an ounce of cannabis, from Henry VIII

An ice cream – a man/geezer (rhyming slang, ice cream freezer).

Hobson's – voice (rhyming slang, Hobson's choice).

Iron – gay man (rhyming slang, iron hoof = poof).

On your Jack – alone (rhyming slang, Jack Jones; also on your Tod, from Tod Sloan).

Jack and Danny – vagina (rhyming slang, fanny).

Jack and Jill – bill (rhyming slang).

Jack and Jills – pills (rhyming slang).

Jack The Ripper – stripper (rhyming slang),

Jacks - £5 (rhyming slang, Jack's Alive).

Jacksie – arse.

Jam jar – car (rhyming slang).

Jam Tart – heart (rhyming slang).

A Janet – a quarter of an ounce of cannabis (rhyming slang, Janet Street-Porter = quarter).

Jig-a-Jig = sex (from pidgin English, hence 'get jiggy with'; see also Zig & Zag = shag)

Jiggle – someone French (rhyming slang, jiggle and jog = frog).

Jivel – a woman (Romany).

Joe – a Pakistani (rhyming slang, Joe Daki)

Johnny Vaughan – porn (rhyming slang).

K - £1,000 (see also bag).

K – Ketamine (also Special K)

Khazi – toilet (see Gary).

Khyber – arse (rhyming slang, Khyber Pass).

A Kim Jong-un – a wrong'un.

Kosher – the real thing.

Linen – newspaper (rhyming slang, linen draper).

Long firm – a business set up and allowed to run over a fairly lengthy period with the sole intention of defrauding creditors.

On the lash – enjoying a drinking session.

Mangled – drunk.

Manor – neighbourhood.

To mark yer cards – to give advice.

Minces – eyes (rhyming slang, mince pies).

Mickey – piss, as in take the piss (rhyming slang Mickey Bliss = piss; also take the Michael).

A monkey – £500.

Moody – fake.

A mug – a stupid person (also Muppet).

To mulla – to beat up.

Mutton – deaf (rhyming slang, Mutt and Jeff)

Ned – TV (rhyming slang, Ned Kelly = telly)

Nigerian Lager – Guinness.

A nonce – child sex offender.

North and south – (rhyming slang, mouth)

Nugget – a £1 coin

Oedipus – sex (rhyming slang, Oedipus Rex; archaic)

Oily – cigarette (rhyming slang, oily rag = fag).

OP – observation post.

Orchestras – testicles (rhyming slang, orchestra stalls = balls)

A parcel – a consignment of stolen goods.

Patsies – piles (rhyming slang, Patsy Palmers = Farmers, Farmer Giles = piles; also Nobbies from Nobby Stiles).

Pet the poodle – female masturbation (also beat the beaver, hit the slit, juice the sluice, bash the gash, slam the clam).

A Peter – a safe.

Pete Tong – wrong (rhyming slang).

Pigs – beer (rhyming slang, pig's ear = beer, usually on George Raft – draft).

Plates – feet (rhyming slang, plates of meat).

Poger – to make love to, aggressively, as in 'I pogered the granny out of her'.

A pony - £25 (also macaroni).

Pony – rubbish (rhyming slang, pony and trap = crap).

Pop – to pawn (rhyming slang, popcorn = porn).

Porkies – lies (rhyming slang, porky pie).

Puff – cannabis (also dope, Bob Hope, grass, blow, wacky baccy, ganja, weed, Beryl Reid, pot, the magic dragon).

Pukka – authentic (see Ream).

Queen Mum – the anus (rhyming slang, Queen Mum = bum; see Aris).

Rabbit – talk (rhyming slang, rabbit and pork).

Raspberry – disabled person (rhyming slang, raspberry ripple = cripple).

Ream – the real thing, or of good quality (see Pukka).

On the Rock 'n' Roll – unemployed (rhyming slang, rock 'n' roll = dole).

Richard = woman (rhyming slang, Richard III = bird, but can also mean turd).

Rosy – tea (rhyming slang, Rosy Lee).

Rubber – pub (rhyming slang, rub-a-dub; see also battle cruiser = boozer).

Ruby – curry (rhyming slang, Ruby Murray = curry).

Salmon – erection (rhyming slang, salmon and prawn = horn; also lob-on).

Saucepan – child (rhyming slang, saucepan lid = kid).

Schnide – fake (see also Sexton Blake).

Score - £20 (see apple).

See You Next Tuesday – a cunt.

Septic – an American (rhyming slang, Septic Tank = yank).

Sexton Blake – counterfeit goods (rhyming slang, Sexton Blake – fake).

A sherbet – a cab (rhyming slang, sherbet dab).

Shovel – jail (rhyming slang, shovel and pail = jail).

Silvery – a black man (rhyming slang, silvery spoon; see also Feargal Sharkey).

Skin and blister – sister (rhyming slang).

Slag – a person with no principles.

Slaphead – a bald man, one who wears the pink crash helmet.

A slaughter – a safe place to dispose of stolen goods, short for slaughter-house.

Smack – heroin (also horse, H, junk, skag, shit, brown, Harry, the white palace, the Chinaman's nightcap.)

A smudger – a photographer.

Sniffer – a reporter (rhyming slang, sniffers and snorters = reporters).

The Spanish Archer – the sack (Spanish archer = El Bow; see also tin-tack = sack).

A sov - £1, from sovereign.

SP – information, from starting prices.

Speed – amphetamines (see Billy)

Spiel – patter.

Squirt – ammonia in a bottle.

A steward's – an investigation, from steward's inquiry.

A stretch – one year in prison.

Strides – trousers.

Stripe – to cut the face with a Frankie or a chiv.

Surrey Docks – syphilis (rhyming slang, Surrey Docks = Pox).

Swagman – a dealer in cheap goods.

Swede – head (see canister).

A syrup – wig (rhyming slang, syrup of figs).

Taters – cold (rhyming slang, taters in the mould; also brass monkeys from 'it's cold enough to freeze the balls off a brass monkey).

Tea-leaf – thief (rhyming slang).

Thrupennies – breasts (rhyming slang, thruppenny bits – tits; see also Earthas, Eartha Kitts, and Bristols, Bristol Cities – titties).

Tiddlies – Chinese people (rhyming slang, tiddly wink).

Tin-Tack – sack (rhyming slang; see also the Spanish Archer – El Bow).

Tits up – to go wrong or pear-shaped.

Tom – jewellery (rhyming slang, tomfoolery).

Tom – defecate (rhyming slang, Tom Tit = shit; see also a Forrest, Forrest Gump = dump).

Tool – a weapon (see April).

VAT – vodka and tonic.

Vera – gin (rhyming slang, Vera Lynn = gin)

Weasel – coat (rhyming slang, weasel and stoat = coat).

A whistle – suit (rhyming slang, whistle and flute = suit).

Wipe his mouth – to put up with the situation.

A Wrong'un – a bad or untrustworthy person.

Wutherings – tights (rhyming slang, Wuthering Heights).

A Yard – £1billion (trader slang, half a yard = £500million.

Yonks – a long time (back slang and rhyming slang, yonky-donks = donkey's ears = years).